ISBN-13: 978-1493799497
ISBN-10: 1493799495

Author website: www.loteyrose.com

The Thirteen of Hearts

Alice peers woefully out the window into the black-and-white squares of Wonderland. When she first arrived here, Wonderland followed the rules of chess, but things changed over the years to a confusing mish mash of broken rules with nonsensical rules piled on top.

It's one of the quiet parts of her days, when the guard card leaves her chained to her writing desk in her hut.

She turns over a card, sets it down onto one of the other cards.

Mumbling to herself, "I will lose again. Like always." Solitaire is a game one rarely wins, she thinks, just like life.

From the edge of her vision, she sees something in the window, causing her to raise her head. One of the male playing cards waves at her next to a scraggly tree in the distance. There are two kinds of cards in

Wonderland—the small kind she plays games with and the person-sized ones with arms and legs and mouths. At first she assumes the card is the Queen of Heart's guard coming to unchain her before her unhappy unbirthday party, but no, it's a different card, one that seems to have holes in it. "Curious," she mumbles to herself, that being one of her favorite one word sentences.

Alice waves back from her desk while smiling huge, though she doesn't recognize the card. He seems to have two vertical lines of holes where symbols should be. She's never before seen a holey card. ("Holey" as in "with holes" not as in "holy cow".)

Though she doesn't recognize him, she assumes it's best to pretend, because she doesn't want to risk offending him, because the citizens of Wonderland can get very cruel when offended.

Alice sighs and returns to her game as the strange card approaches. She hopes he's nice, or at least the amusements he seeks are not too vicious.

Soon, there is a knock at the door.

She shouts, "Come in! I'm a bit chained to my desk at the moment!"

The door opens, and there stands the large card, ogling her from the doorway.

She ogles back, for he is a most curious card, unlike any she's ever seen before. Because the light behind him shoots beams of light through the heart-shaped holes in his body that are lined up in two columns like an ordinary playing card. But there, centered above the columns is another cut-out heart, which is quite abnormal.

Quickly she counts the cut-out hearts. Six on the left, six on the right, plus the one on top…

The answer comes as a shout from the card, as if it's a playful race. "Thirteen!" he proclaims, raising his short arms up in the air and flourishing with a little hop. "I am the Thirteen of Hearts. Or, the twelvety-one of them, if you prefer."

Alice makes a wrinkly face. "How can you fit so many wrong things in such a short utterance?"

"Is that a riddle?" He clasps his hands together in front of him in a mocking sort of delight. "Here's one!" His eyes ping to the wooden seat she's chained to. "Why is a raven like a writing desk?"

She rolls her eyes, despite the fact she doesn't yet know how easily offended, and just how cruel he can be. Note, she doesn't wonder *if* he is cruel, but *how much* of that quality he possesses, for it has been her experience that most of the creatures of Wonderland are cruel now. They started out as pleasant or tolerable, but they've grown downright malicious over the past six years. They've quite forgotten the rules of civility, and even the rules of Wonderland, what little there were to begin with, it seems to her. One of the few exceptions is the Jabberwock, who seems nice, but shy.

After she rolls her eyes, she says, "Yes I've heard that riddle before so many times, and I have so many answers, depending on the situation, because I've had so much time to think on it, chained here, you see. But let's not go to that right now. Let's go back to what you said. So many things are wrong with it, it makes me quite see red." She looks at him hopefully, hoping he will appreciate her flight of poetry. She's acquired a habit of rhyming whenever she can, being after all a (unwilling) citizen of Wonderland.

The card takes two steps into the hut, with its bed, and books laid page down on the ground, its stove in the far corner, its small dining table where they set her cakes during her unhappy unbirthday parties, its painting on the wall of Alice's parents.

The card takes two more steps, looks around, now at her, and says, "What's the second thing you dislike about what I said?"

Alice doesn't even bother to groan out loud and huff. *All* the creatures of Wonderland are just like this—so clever, whimsical, full of mischief. "The second thing," she says, "is that there is no such number as 'twelvety-one'. But the *first* thing is that you are quite lacking in hearts, so it is wrong to say you're the Thirteen of Hearts, because you have holes where hearts would be. You're actually heart*less.*"

He says, "And who do *you* say you are?"

"I'm Alice. I don't believe we have met." She holds out her unchained hand—her left one. She happens to be left-handed.

The card shakes hands, then bows. "Nice to meet you. Yes, this is my first day of existence. I'm an entirely new card. Depending on which card game you're playing, if you were to draw me, why, I'd completely change the game! I am a surprise card you see. A wild card! More wild than the joker! I see that you are playing solitaire. Why, if you were to draw me, do you know what the rule would be?"

"Why no. As you say, you're new. I've never encountered a card such as you in a deck."

The card stands up straight and regally, and proclaims,

"If solitaire's the game that you draw me in,
Up into the air, toss five darts!
If one of them sticks in the ceiling, you win!
For I am the Thirteen of Hearts!"

In annoyance, she shouts, "Less!"

The card, looking somewhat deflated at Alice's lack of being impressed, says, "No, I assure you, I'm thirteen *exactly*. No more. No less."

"Well I'm thirteen too, more or less."

Now he peers at her body, as if *she* is the curious creature!

Alice, ignoring his rude eyes, says, "What I *meant* is you're not the Thirteen of Hearts, for you only have empty spaces where hearts would go! So as I said before, it's more accurate to say you're heart*less!*"

"Yes!" he shouts, with a big grin. Now another bow, this time with a twirly whirl of his arm as he bends downward.

"If me you are dealt when poker's the game,
Your opponents must fold then confess,
The one thing they feel is their own greatest shame,
Because I'm the Thirteen of Hearts...LESS!"

He twirls in a little circle, coming back around to face her.

Alice says, "No. No. *Heart*less. That's the proper way of pronouncing it."

The card rolls his eyes, crosses his arms. "That's not how you said it before. And why are you such an expert anyway? What exactly are *you* the thirteen of?" He leans forward slightly, staring at her body and black dress. "I see no marks on you. No spades, no diamonds, clubs... or hearts! No *heart*lesses either, I might add."

"Well," says Alice, "I'm not a card, I'm a girl, twelve years old you see, almost thirteen."

The card says, "Today's your birthday."

Alice gasps. "Why so it is! I had totally forgotten. Imagine that! How did you know it was my birthday?"

"Well, I was at the party. Weren't you invited?"

Alice pouts. "No, I wasn't. Who hosted it?"

"Why the Queen of Hearts, of course. She's the one who took all my hearts!"

6

"Ah, I see. I'm so sorry."

The card frowns. "Me too. Did she take your hearts too? I see none on you."

"Well, I don't have one *on* me."

"So you're a one of heartlesses?"

"No, I have a heart, but it's inside, so you can't see it right now. And I'm not sure your saying 'heartlesses' is correct, for heartlessness is not a thing but an absence of a thing, so I can't see how it can be plural."

The card makes big eyes and points to himself while waving his arm up and down. "You're obviously wrong, for look, I have thirteen heartlesses."

Alice rubs her chin. "Why, I see you do. Perhaps I'm incorrect. I wonder, if I got rid of my own heart, which has caused me so much pain, would I be a 'one of heartless'?"

"Heartless!" the card proclaims. "Why…"

Now he starts to dance a little, bending up and down, pumping an imaginary bicycle pump with his arms.

"Let's say you're dealt me, when it's blackjack you play,
And your age is before drinking starts, yes?
Well, you'll be 21 for exactly one day.
The power of Thirteen of Heartless!"

Alice scowls. "But what's that got to do with the game? Would I win or lose?"

"Why, what does it matter? You wouldn't care either way if it was the first time you imbibed. Have you ever gotten drunk?"

Alice narrows her eyes disapprovingly. She does her best to cross her arms, though they don't quite cross all the way due to her right arm still being chained to her desk. "I'm thirteen." She rolls her eyes.

The card mimics her posture, right down to the awkwardly angled right arm. "Of?…"

She sighs in frustration. "Nothing! I'm just a girl. I'm not a card like you."

He lowers his arms, looking genuinely perplexed. "But I recall you saying you were a one of hearts. Red or black?"

She thinks for a moment of correcting him once again, but instead ponders a bit, says woefully, "Black. I have a black heart. From living in this horrible place, all these years."

Now the card, taking his cue from her, seems woeful as well. "I'm sorry. But I doubt you have a black heart. You seem too nice. It must be terrible to be the 'one' of anything. I didn't even know the numbers went so low."

She lowers her arms. "Well, it is the average number of hearts to have for my sort, which is human girls. But let me tell you, this one heart of mine has been the source of such great misery, for it forces me to feel all that happens to me, and provides me only yearning and loneliness and sadness."

"Those are three things."

"Pardon?"

"You said 'only' then you listed three things."

Alice sighs. "You wouldn't understand. You're only a card. I say 'only' because they are empty things, you see. Oh, I wish I could be heartless like you."

The card hops, then twirls in midair. "Well, why don't you be? How hard can it be to get rid of your heart?" He does a little dance. "Why, you only have one, after all!"

Alice pouts. "But us girls need our hearts! We couldn't live without them."

"Ah, but this is Wonderland! Why, look at me! I am the Thirteen of Heartless! You should be like me! I break all the rules. I'm a renegade. I was created to make Wonderland more interesting, to shake things up, for I'm a wild card! Why, I can even show up anywhere in the deck I want to!"

"Isn't that cheating?"

"Absolutely!"

Alice bites her lip in frustration. She's heard of players of cards cheating, but not the actual cards themselves. "So who created you?"

"Why no one did! I'm your birthday present! I popped out of a big cake at your birthday party!"

"But that makes no sense. Who put you *in* the cake?"

"Why, no one did!"

"But you can't pop out of a cake unless you first go in!"

"Well that sounds like a rule, and I don't follow rules!"

Alice sighs. "Did the Queen have fun at my party?" Usually whenever anyone says, "the Queen", they are referring to the Queen of Hearts, because the Red Queen doesn't get mentioned as much, due to the fact that she's currently locked up in the Queen of Heart's dungeon.

The card says, "Yes, unfortunately. I'd just like to say it was rather rude for you not to show up for your own birthday party. Oh, but Queen had fun beheading people and creatures. 'Off with their heads!' she kept saying." He's scowling now.

Alice hates the Queen of Hearts, because she's responsible for so much of the misery in Alice's life. It is the Queen's guard who keeps Alice chained up, who forces her to go on her daily rounds—rounds in which the Tweedle twins like to make her cry so they can lick her tears, the Caterpillar makes her smoke from his hookah, and the Queen herself uses Alice's tears to make herself more beautiful. Alice says, "And what happened to your hearts?"

"I had to give them to the Queen, because she collects them. She's a thief who stole my hearts! I wish I could get back at her. But I must admit, it's so much more fun being heartless. Why, I can be ruthless and vicious, a cad, a renegade! And not care a whit, for I have not even one heart!"

"I envy you. My only one heart is quite a burden. I would like to try being heartless, but just for a little while. Can you help me?"

"Why certainly my dear! I'd love to make another heartless being like me, to help me get revenge on the Queen! And I think you may grow to like it, though you say only 'a little while'." He winks. "I shall simply make a rule!"

"But I thought you liked to break rules!"

He waves his hand dismissively. "Pish posh. Why my dear, whenever I *make* a new rule, I *break* the old rules. It's all the same."

Alice thinks about this. "Yes, I suppose that's true."

"So I shall simply make a rule that lets you take out your heart, and put it back in if you want!" He beams as if supremely proud of himself.

"You can simply make up rules? Pull them out of thin air?"

"Yes, like pulling a rabbit from a hat! Magic!" He makes razzle dazzle jazz hands.

The joy at possibly achieving her goal causes Alice to beam, herself. "So what's the rule?"

Now the card is waggling a finger. "Oh, no. There can be no rule unless the game is known. What card game do you propose?"

"Solitaire."

"There's already a rule for that, silly. I just recited it to you a few moments ago."

"Can't there be another one?"

"No! Only one rule per game. I thought that was obvious."

"Well it wasn't obvious to me, so no it wasn't. But how about Old Maid?"

"Already a rule. Would you like to hear it?"

"No thank you. How about Go Fish? Hearts? Um…"

"No there are already rules for those. I've been thinking of rules all day, and none of them have to do with you getting rid of your heart."

Alice is annoyed. "So why don't you tell me a game you don't have a rule for yet."

"Well, that would be difficult, for you see, I've made a rule for every card game I can think of, so in order to suggest one, I'd have to think of one I can't think of, which would be most difficult."

Alice thinks the creatures of Wonderland can be so very irritating, but she rarely does anything, because she is so nice. And she would definitely never do anything to hurt them, though she's often felt that if she could bring herself to harm some of her tormentors she might make a better life for herself, but then again, they might strike back, making things worse than before, so maybe not. Even so, she wants to try being heartless just a little while, but this card is not making things easy. Frustrated, she says, "Well, I say, this hat that you've been pulling rules out of seems to be quite empty!"

Now what she just said stirs something in her mind. She says, "What about the game of 'Tossing Cards in a Hat'?" She doesn't know if it counts as a card game, since it is more of a throwing game, and also, she doesn't have a hat, but even so, it would be a minor victory to think of something that the Thirteen of Heartless had not.

"Aha!" he says, lifting a finger in the air. "I had not thought of that."

"So there's no rule?"

"Of course not! But come now I shall make one.

"If you play someone who also may win,
And you toss me in a hat far away,
You can take out your heart, or put it back in.
For I'm the Thirteen of Heartless, I say!"

Alice is excited, tries to clap, but she is still chained. So now she kind of taps her right hand with her left. Now she remembers though—"But I haven't got a hat!"

"Well you need one to play."

"How about a different card game? One I can play now?"

"Oh, no, I won't waste all those rules just for you. You'll just have to find a hat."

And now they hear, coming through the walls on the right side of Alice, a bunch of yowling and hooting. They are coming, as they do every day at noon. They must have forgotten it's her birthday too. To the card she explains, "It's my surprise unhappy unbirthday party."

"You don't look very surprised."

"Well the surprise part comes in the various ways they torment me during each party. They try something new every day."

"Well why do you let them do that? Why, if it were me, I'd show them a thing or two."

"Because I'm not really a mean person. They say I wouldn't hurt a fly. They said that a month ago, when to prove it, they taped my wrists, covered me in glue and put a piece of raw meat on top of my head. You can imagine the result." She shudders.

The card laughs. "Yes, very funny! So shall we play toss me in a hat?"

"No, I haven't got a hat…but the Mad Hatter does. He'll be one of my guests. But I must say, you're a bit big for me to toss anyhow. You wouldn't fit in his hat."

"So I'll shrink!"

And with that, the card leaps and shrinks in midair to the size of one of Alice's hand-sized playing cards. It balances precariously on the edge of the desk for a second before she grabs it, gathers all the cards together, then slips the deck into a pocket of her black dress. Many dresses don't have pockets, but hers does, and the pockets have the amazing ability to hold huge amounts without causing a bulge.

She slips the deck in as her first guest appears in her doorway, without having to open it, for the door has remained open this whole time.

Unhappy Unbirthday!

The first of them to walk in is Tweedledum, carrying the chocolate unbirthday cake—it's always the same flavor—with always twelve candles that could not be blown out, though they always made her try, while they laughed. Tweedledum says, "Unhappy unbirthday."

Tweedledee comes in next. He says, "Ditto." He's carrying a large rolled up piece of paper. Tweedledum and Tweedledee look like two chubby twin boys.

Humpty Dumpty enters next, as they all begin to sing. He has his razorblade he likes to cut Alice with. But thankfully he's not carrying the tape. She hates when he brings the tape.

"Unhappy unbirthday to you!" they all sing.

The March Hare comes in next while they sing, carrying the Dormouse, who is sound asleep, in his arms. The Dormouse looks kind of like a mouse with a furry tail, and he always seems to be sleeping.

"Unhappy unbirthday to you!"

Next through the door is the Mad Hatter, carrying two custard pies—one in each hand.

"Unhappy unbirthday, pathetic Alice!"

Next comes the Three of Hearts. It's his job to unchain Alice every day so she can go on her appointed rounds. He doesn't follow her throughout the day though—she's allowed to go on her rounds by herself, because everyone knows Alice is trustworthy to a fault.

Behind the guard, squeezing through the doorway, galumphs the Jabberwock, the only one of them not singing. He has to stoop so as not to hit the ceiling—either he's somewhat too big for the room, or the room is somewhat too small. He's holding his vorpal sword in one of his clawed hands. She's heard that he guards one of the eighth squares where the Looking Glass House is located, and he only leaves to attend her parties every day.

"Unhappy unbirthday to you!"

The guard card uses his key to unlock her as Tweedledum sets the cake on the table. They never let her eat any of the cake. They always eat it themselves.

As Alice approaches the table, they all clap, except for the Jabberwock, who is standing apart at the end of the room. Watching. He always just watches. He's never mean, like the others. She often feels sorry for him, because she suspects he's forced to tag along due to peer pressure. And she suspects that, despite the rumors, he never stole the Queen of Heart's tarts—he just seems too nice to do a thing like that.

Humpty says, "Blow out the candles, or I'll cut you!" He slashes the blade through the air, almost striking the March Hare, who yelps. "Careful with that thing. You almost woke him," he says, referring to the Dormouse.

"Well you shouldn't stand in the way!" Humpty explains.

The Tweedle twins are now shouting, "Blow out the candles!" They snicker.

It is a tradition and expected of her, and she hates to disappoint. So she does what she does every single day and blows out the candles. There is a pause while the creatures watch, then the flames pop back up.

They all laugh at her.

Alice smiles and tries to appear gracious.

Tweedledee says, "Are you ready for your prize?" He unfurls a large paper cut-out replica of Alice. "Ta da!" He heads for one of the walls.

Alice announces, "However, today is not my unbirthday."

Humpty Dumpty shakes his head gravely. "You shouldn't start a sentence with 'however' unless you have a sentence stating something appropriate before, which would be the thing you're howevering. It's not grammatical. I should cut you."

"Sorry," Alice says, curtsying. "I mean to say, today is actually my birthday, so it's the wrong day for this party."

Various of the creatures say things, after gasping, such as:

"Is it true?"

"Whose fault is this?"

"How can it be?"

And, "How rude!"

"Inappropriate!"

"I'm very sorry," says Alice, but "I'm sure tomorrow will be my unbirthday again. We could have a surprise party then!"

The Mad Hatter puts on a most pitiful face, it brings such guilt to Alice. Woefully, he says, "But I was going to smash these pies in your face."

From the end of the room, Tweedledee says, "And we were going to play pin the tail on the Alice." He had set the paper replica of Alice on the wall without her noticing. "And everywhere we pinned the tail, we would actually stick *you* with a pin." He sighs. "It would have been so funny."

Next to him, Tweedledum says, "Ditto" in a sad sad voice.

Alice says, "Do you have a blindfold?"

Tweedledum says, "Of course not! How would we be able to see where we stick the pins?" He crosses his arms.

"I'm sorry. I didn't mean to offend you."

The March Hare says to Alice, "Why didn't you say anything before?"

The Dormouse lifts his head, says, "I'm sorry, but I was taking a nap." He lowers his head again and closes his eyes.

Alice opens her mouth to speak, but the Mad Hatter interrupts her by saying, "Well, I suppose we should be leaving then! I take it you will be going on your usual rounds?"

Alice nods. "Yes, I expect so."

They all turn to leave, all except the guard, who must stay to inform her of her duties for the day.

Alice suddenly remembers a custom that may help her get access to the Mad Hatter's hat, though.

She shouts, "No, wait! My birthday wish! I'd like to ask it of you, Hatter."

They all turn back around again. The Hatter looks quite put out—he is still holding the two pies in his hands—they look rather precariously balanced and heavy after being held for so long.

Alice says, "But I want to let you win at a game!"

She's hoping the Hatter won't start asking too many questions.

Thankfully, his eyebrow twerks up. "Oh? I enjoy winning games. What kind of game?"

"Toss the Card in the Hat. As I said, I'll let you win and the winner, well, the winner gets to smash those pies in the loser's face. Please play wif me?" She gives her best big doe-eyed pathetic expression.

A predatory grin comes across his face. "Yes, that expression! Wear exactly that expression when I smash the pies in your face, won't you?"

She nods with a cute pout.

But some of the others are grumbling.

Tweedledum says, "Hey, how about us?"

Tweedledee says, "Don't we get to play?"

The Hatter shouts, "Silence! She's the birthday girl, and it is her wish to play with just me, because I'm special, right?"

Alice says, "Yes. Just the Hatter."

There is more groaning.

The Hatter says, "So what are the rules?" He sets the pies down. "Oh, my arms! I held those things this whole time!"

"Well, the rules are that the winner is the person who doesn't toss the card in the hat after the other player does. Do you think you can win at such a game?"

The Hatter stands thinking for several long moments, his eyes rolled toward the ceiling. He seems to be mouthing many of the words of the rules she'd stated. "Ah, I believe I have devised a brilliant strategy to win this game! Let us begin."

"Okay. I have a special card to play with. It has holes in it so it can fly through the air."

The Dormouse shouts, "Aerodynamic!" then promptly goes back to sleep.

"That's right," Alice says. "Who goes first?"

"Ladies first, because I am a gentleman," says the Hatter. He removes his top hat.

So Alice tries her best to toss the card into the hat. It barely misses.

The Hatter gives the card a meager fling then laughs. "I am the most clever hatter in Wonderland!" he proclaims. He is also the maddest. They say he's gone mad from all the mercury and chemicals he uses to make his hats—all the noxious substances make beautiful hats, but are quite toxic.

It takes several tries, but finally Alice manages to toss the card in the hat. "Well, guess I lose!" she says, before lifting the card from the hat.

The Hatter puts his own hat on, with a tap on the top.

Alice looks down discreetly to see that the card is glowing. *Should I take my heart out now? But how?*

"I've a surprise!" she shouts. "Everyone close your eyes! Keep them closed!"

While everyone closes their eyes, she presses her hand into her chest, which is a strange thing to do, and pulls out her heart. It looks like a cartoonish heart, colored bright red. There is no blood or pain, but that seems perfectly normal in Wonderland. "Wait, wait! I've almost got it ready. Don't open your eyes!" She quickly runs and puts the heart inside a wooden jewelry box. While she is doing so, she feels like Humpty Dumpty is peeking at her, but when she glances at him, his eyes are closed.

She goes back to stand by the table. In a panic she lifts the two pies and holds them toward the Mad Hatter. "Okay! Open your eyes! Ta da!"

The reactions are mixed. Some cheer and applaud, some boo and express disapproval. She admits, it's not much of a surprise, but it's the best she could think of.

What a bunch of decrepit characters, she thinks.

"Shall I pie you now?" says the Hatter.

Alice nods. Even though she doesn't want to, she thinks it would be best not to arouse suspicion, so she puts on her doe-eyed pathetic expression and she stands still and willing as the Hatter smashes not one, but two pies in her face.

Everyone laughs but her.

I wonder how the bastard would like a pie smashed in his face?

As she's wiping the custard from her face, the Hatter informs her that he has more pies waiting to use on her when next she visits him at the tea table.

They all begin leaving, except for the card guard. Alice waves. She doesn't say goodbye, because many of them expect her to visit them sometime during the day. The Tweedle twins wish her an "Unhappy birthday," which makes her want to strangle them, but she just grins and bears it.

Finally it is just her and the guard card in the room. It's the same card guard card as usual. He stays after each party to provide her list of scheduled duties, and he is a total idiot. She thinks it's maybe because he's only the number three, or maybe it's because he's so flat, and not much brain matter can be fit in such a flat surface. He has been the source of much of her sorrow, and she wants to get revenge.

The cake is still there, flickering with its candles, forgotten.

"Guard card," she says, cooingly. "It's my birthday, so I'd like you to do the customary thing and blow my candles out." She feels a thrill go through her. Never before has she been able to engage in the level of deception she intends in the next few moments.

"What? Why would I blow the candles out? It's *your* unhappy unbirthday!"

"Idiot! It's my *birthday*. Haven't you been paying attention? The rules are the opposite today. *I* don't blow the candles out, *you* do."

"I do? The Queen didn't mention anything about that. Besides, the candles are blowproof—they can't be blown out."

"Wow, how dumb are you? Must the Queen tell you everything? Everything is the opposite today. The candles are the opposite of unblowable, because it's my birthday, not my unbirthday. Wow, just how dumb are you?" Alice had never been so deceptive before. It's a good skill to have, she thinks.

The card says, "But I just saw you try to blow them out a while ago. They went out and came back again."

"Moron! That was a few moments ago! And that was me, not you. The candles can only be blown out by you, not me, because this is my birthday, and not my unbirthday! How dumb are you?" She hopes she is being sufficiently confusing. She fights the urge to chuckle.

She watches the card ponder what she said, or at least *try* to. He nods. "Okay." He leans down and blows the candles out. He grins at her.

The candles spring back into flame.

Alice shouts, "Idiot! You have to lean closer!"

"Closer? But—"

"Closer! Moron! Imbecile! Buffoon! Do it!"

The card leans closer than before, blows the candles out. He grins at her.

The candles burst back into flame.

"Closer closer closer! Do you not know the meaning of the word? Don't make me tell you again!"

This time the card leans very close indeed, but before he even has the chance to blow, he catches fire, and begins flailing about while screaming, but the flails only make the flames grow higher.

Alice merely watches while laughing and pointing at him.

The card now lies as an ashy burnt smoking remnant of the card, now quite dead.

She digs the keys to her chains from the ashes then slips the chains and keys in her pocket.

When she goes to the jewelry box, she finds that her heart is missing.

Someone has stolen it!

Her thoughts turn dark, filled with ideas of revenge.

No one steals something from me, unpunished! I'll find out who did it, and I will make their life, or death, pure hell!

And first on her list of suspects is Humpty Dumpty. Her mind fills with the delicious fantasy of chaining Humpty Dumpty and torturing him to punish him for stealing her heart.

The Cheshire Cat

Tra la la la la la la.

She hops and skips wickedly.

Things are definitely different with me.

Why, just yesterday, my black dress symbolized my brooding melancholy and now it shows my malevolence and duplicity.

She's smugly satisfied with the words she had chosen—they were quite impressive in their number of syllables.

They show how much smarter I am than the average girl.

She stops when she hears the familiar purr in her right ear.

The Cheshire Cat.

"Kill yourself," he whispers, as usual. He swoops out to face her, floating in front of her.

He's a floating, grinning cat head with no body.

Alice tries her best not to glare him down evilly. She puts on the meek face she usually greets him with.

The Cheshire Cat says, "You've thought of my offer, I can tell."

Yes, his offer. His offer is this: he will provide her with a pistol, if only she agrees to shoot herself in the head with it.

She never accepted though and the cat knows if she ever *did* accept she would follow through, for all the creatures of Wonderland know she is incapable of lying.

That is, I was until today.

The pistol pops into view, floating, glowing in the air next to the cat's head. It is a single shot, flintlock pistol, with an ivory handle and a single lead ball bullet inside—a dueling pistol. "Why not take it?" he says.

She ignores his offer, offers instead, "I'm searching for something that was just stolen from me. Have you heard anything about it?"

"No, I've heard nothing. What was stolen?"

It's best for others to still think she's sweet and caring she thinks, so she says, "I don't want to say exactly what. I just want to know if you know anything about it? Do you know who might have it?"

He just grins that stupid grin. "You're teasing me. But I forgive you because you're so pretty."

Her shoulders slump. "Thank you."

"Awww. If I help you get this thing back, will you kill yourself as my reward?"

"Yes." She nods and nods eagerly. She'd never really lied before today. It feels somehow thrilling. Had she been missing this feeling all her life?

"Such a pretty girl, so pretty on the inside too. I would love to see your brains."

"Thank you." She decides to lie even more. "I tell you what, if you let me have the pistol, I promise I'll shoot myself very soon if I can't find the object I'm looking for. But if I *do* get the object back, I'll be so happy that I'll kill myself so I can die happy. So can I have the gun, pleeeeaaase?"

The cat looks at her suspiciously. "Well…why do you need it? I'll just give it to you when the time comes."

"Awwww Mister Puss Puss. Don't you trust me?"

Everyone trusts Alice, or the old one with her heart intact.

"Well, everyone knows you can't lie. It's a weakness of yours. As long as you promise me…"

She looks at him innocently and protrudes her bottom lip. "I pwomise, cross my heart and hope to die, I'll kill myself very soon, if you just give me the pistol."

He relaxes and his grin edges up again. "Okay, but promise not to do it without letting me watch okay?"

She gives him thumbs up. "Promise!"

The cat giggles. "I'm so glad you finally decided to give in. Here's the pistol. It's a single shot dueling pistol, so aim carefully so you don't miss." He laughs. "That's a little joke. I'm implying you have a tiny brain."

Alice smiles to keep from scowling. "Very funny."

"Yes, it was. Well, here you go."

He mouths her the pistol. "Now, I must be off, because I'm bored with talking to you. Oh, I get bored so easily."

He vanishes.

She slips the pistol into her dress. It could come in very handy for her mission.

TweedleduM and TweedleDee

Alice is headed for Humpty's place, but the Tweedles' place is along the way. Even from quite a distance, she hears them bickering. She rolls her eyes

Hmmm, only one bullet in the gun. Perhaps if I lined them up properly...

She grins at the wicked thought. Before, whenever she thought of killing them, she would mentally scold herself. But now she enjoys the thought.

It might be easy to line them up, since they are so often mirroring each other's movements.

She'll take a slight detour, she decides, to visit the twins.

They're standing in a clearing beneath the shade of an oak tree.

As usual, they're circling a toy rattle on the ground, grimacing and taunting each other. The squabble has gone on for quite a number of years, ever since the Queen of Hearts rewarded them a brand new rattle for helping her defeat the Red Queen.

Tweedledum glares at his brother and proclaims, "Mine!"

"Nohow!" says Tweedledee.

They continue circling and seem not to notice Alice as she takes the pistol out from her dress.

She takes a stance in the way she remembers from detective stories as a younger child.

She braces one hand with the other and does her best to aim with the little shark fin thingy on the edge of the bullet tube part.

But she encounters several problems. For one, she is not tall enough to get a clear head shot of either one of them, and her lack of height makes a *double* head shot impossible, due to the working of angles. She has studied angles a great deal, and knows that out of all of them, none of them would work, at least not without a ricochet.

Also, they are moving so rapidly, round and round in a circle, that it's difficult to get any kind of clear shot, inexperienced as she is.

Perhaps she could aim for one of their hearts. As far as she knows, even though they are both vicious and cruel to her, they both have hearts. But pulling that kind of shot off seems difficult indeed. And maybe they don't even have hearts after all.

She begins to realize her situation is dire and dreadful. Even if she manages to kill one of them, she would afterward be unarmed and suffer the wrath of the other, and that would not be a fair fight—she's just a little girl.

She thinks she'll put the gun away. Perhaps she can slip away without being noticed. They haven't noticed her this whole time standing here, pointing a gun at them, after all.

She begins to lower the gun. She notices her hands are trembling from fear. It appears being heartless doesn't mean you don't get afraid.

But Tweedledum notices her, stops circling, points. "Well look at that! It's Alice!"

Now Tweedledee stops and turns to look at her. "Well, ditto! It is! And she has a toy pistol!"

Thank goodness he thinks it's a toy. "Yes…" She musters up a grin on her face. "A toy! I brought you a new toy!"

Tweedledum says, "Well give it over. I know how to use it. Better than *him.*"

Alice doubts that statement. They both seem generally bumbling and incompetent to her.

Tweedledee protests, "Nohow! I'm a cowboy I am!" He grabs his belt and does the side to side cowboy hop. "Yee haw!"

Tweedledum grunts. "Yeehaw! He's no cowboy, nohow, no way. Why I'm a sharpshooter. Cool and professional. A sharpshooter you see, remains calm and collected and never says yeehaw…unless it's to mock, which I just did right then. So give the gun to me and ignore this yahoo."

"Nohow!" Tweedledee protests.

Alice does her best to steady her nerves.

She doesn't know how she is going to get out of this most troubling predicament. She opts to distract them for a few moments. "Patience! First thing's first, I'm searching for something that got stolen from me. By Humpty Dumpty, I suspect."

Now they are nodding at her, both saying "Ditto. We saw the idiot doing it."

"Well why didn't you stop him?"

Tweedledum shrugs. "Why would we? He was only stealing from *you.*"

Alice fights back the urge to put a bullet right into the middle of his pudgy, scrunchy face.

Tweedledee says, "Ditto on that. You're so unimportant, it doesn't matter. What did he steal anyway? We didn't see."

Tweedledum says, "Ditto to not seeing."

Her voice quivers with rage. "He stole my heart!"

They both stand looking a bit perplexed, then dumbfounded, then at exactly the same time, they burst out laughing. "Is that all? So you're heartless now, is that it?"

With a look of indignation, she nods.

Tweedledum says, "So are you no longer the goody two shoes?"

"Yeah, no longer a doormat? Are you going to get revenge on us, is that it?"

She shrugs.

"Ditto! Revenge of the little girl!" More laughter.

Their faces suddenly turn mean. "Just know, that if you try anything, it's…" At the same time, they both make the gesture of slicing the throat with the accompanying sound.

"If you're lucky we'll kill you. If not, we'll torture you, or tell the Queen and *she'll* torture you and she's much more imaginative than us."

"Ditto. She's like an artist of torture."

They glare at her and cross their arms, daring her to speak.

"You already torture me."

She's referring to the twins' playtime she's forced to engage in. They have set times each day when she must visit them. They like to make her kneel and then either slap her or tickle her until she cries. Before she came to Wonderland, she never knew that tickling could be a source of such misery. And while they do these things to her, she has to remain as still as possible, until the tears come. Then the twins like to lick her tears, each one licking from one of her eyes. The twins think they're delicious and also believe the rumor that her tears are magical, as does the Queen, who likes to spritz her face with them as a beauty treatment.

Tweedledum says, "We merely have a little fun. We haven't *really* tried to hurt you."

"Ditto. So don't get any ideas in your head."

Alice swallows nervously. She's starting to realize that maybe it hadn't been the best idea to tell them her heart had been stolen. But she is so unused to being deceptive. If she had just acted like she was the usual Alice, maybe this conversation wouldn't be happening.

She decides to play it meek. "Okay, I'm not going to try anything. I'll be good." She doesn't want to draw the wrath of the Queen or the twins.

"Very good. A well behaved girl is something to treasure. So let's test how obedient you are."

Alice sounds resigned. "Shall it be tickling or slapping this time?"

"Neither nohow. This time we'll do a little hair-tugging and shaking."

"Yes, we'll put your hair in pigtails and tug them until you cry!"

"Okay," Alice says, "just please show a little mercy, and I'll do whatever you want."

Tweedledee says, "You better, or suffer a spanking."

"Whap whap!" says Tweedledum.

She lowers her head meekly. "But before that, if I may ask a quick question. When Humpty Dumpty left the party, I didn't see the heart on him. Did he take it with him? I'd very much like to get it back, you see."

They both shrug. "We don't know, maybe he put it inside himself!"

The other brother laughs at the idea. "Why, he could make a heartegg omelet! Get it? It's like 'heartache'!"

"There's not much to get," says the other brother.

Alice says, "What is inside of Humpty Dumpty in actuality? He always claims he is most definitely *not* an egg." She has never before given the idea serious thought, because in the past, whenever she would think of Humpty's insides, it would be accompanied by fantasies of him falling off his wall and dying so he would no longer be able to torment her. But the thoughts troubled her so, that she tried to put them out of her mind. Until now.

Tweedledee says, "Well whether he is or is not an egg is a subject of debate, but inside, if you were ever to actually look, you would not find any egg material."

Alice says, "What a curious answer. What do you mean? Do you know for certain what's inside him?"

Tweedledee says, "We do now. See I used to assume that there were eggs inside him as well, but you can't always judge someone's insides by what you see on the exterior."

Tweedledum says, "Yes, yes, sometimes when you look too hard inside others, you only end up seeing yourself."

Alice was having a hard time understanding these puzzling statements. "Are we still talking about Humpty Dumpty? So he doesn't have egg inside?"

"No, of course not. Didn't I already say that?" Tweedledee says. "I know because I found out first hand."

Alice's eyes go wide in wonder. "How come you never told me?"

"You never asked. Have you never heard our poem? It is a wonderful poem. You should have asked earlier."

She shakes her head. "Yes, well before, I found it too unpleasant to think about!"

"Okay, in any case, here's the poem.

Humpty Dumpty sat on a wall.
Humpty Dumpty had a great fall.
But it turns out that fall, it was more of a shove,
To make a cheese omelet, a dish we both love.

Beware though, if from him, a meal you will make,
You must check the yolk. There is so much at stake!
For if you just rush, and don't stop for a minute,
You'll end up with too much of your *own* self within it.

See, Tweedle *him* and Tweedle *me*,
We learned this lesson personally,
And had to sort and glue what the *one* had broken,
While the *other one* had not yet woken.

And just as the poem comes to a close, she feels the other brother grab her arm from behind. She hadn't been paying attention and he had snuck up behind her.

He puts pulls her arm while making a grab for the pistol. But Alice squirms away. "Keep away!" she shouts. She runs a few steps, stops.

"I want that pistol!" Tweedledum shouts as he comes toward her.

Tweedledee shouts, "Ditto!"

Alice shouts, "Well, then fetch!" She tosses the pistol to the ground, in what she judges to be an equal distance between either twin.

The twins look at each other, then at the same time, run toward the gun.

They manage to each knock the other over, in front of the pistol. Then they begin taunting and grimacing again, circling the pistol.

"Mine!" shouts Tweedledee.

"Quite to the contrary! It is *mine.*" Tweedledum shouts back.

As the two squabble over the pistol, circling it now while snarling at each other, with their hands crinkled out like they're about to start a wrestling match, Alice grabs the rattle and slips it into her dress pocket.

Wretched thing! If they can't decide between themselves who shall play with it then it shall be neither! For shame, it is but a child's toy anyhow!

They don't seem to notice as she slips away.

HUMPTY DUMPTY

Alice holds the rattle to her ear, and gives it a shake with a demoniacal grin.

Perhaps it might have amused me a while when I first got here at the tender age of seven, but it's nothing to me now that I'm thirteen. It's hardly a trifle worthy of fighting over, but the Tweedles have always been rather simple. Perhaps one will end up shooting the other with the pistol. Good riddance. I would have found it most difficult to kill them both at once, and if I killed only one, the other would surely seek revenge.

Her next stop is Humpty Dumpty's wall. It isn't far from where the Tweedles dwell.

As she approaches, she can hear him singing to himself, over and over to himself.

"I'm Humpty Dumpty, here on my wall!
I'm Humpty Dumpty, and I cannot fall!"

Soon, she is standing in front of him.

There he is sitting on his very narrow, really quite low wall. (It's only three bricks thick, three feet wide, and only a few inches taller than Alice herself.) He used to have a higher and wider one, but the Queen took it away and gave him this one after he offended her in some way a few years ago.

Alice waves hyperactively at him, with a goofy grin on her face. "Hello egghead!"

She'd only ever called him that once, as a sort of joke when she was eight. He'd laughed along with her, asked her to come closer, then surprised her with a kick to her face that bloodied her nose and knocked her backward onto her rear.

Do you remember, Humpty-so-grumpy?

"What is this?" he asks, then chuckles a little. Now he laughs, now he outright *guffaws* with thundering belly laughs, teetering back and forth precariously on his very narrow wall. And for a moment Alice is filled with hope that he will fall, but of course he never does. "That's funny!" he shouts. "But you know what's even funnier? Come closer, child, and I shall tell you!"

Alice puts on a darling girl smile, sweet as can be, with dimples and all. She twirls and curtsies, raising the bottom edge of her black dress. "No thank you. No offense, right? I'm just joking with you."

But Humpty Dumpty, she knows, is a very non-joking sort. He's quite vicious and cruel. The great curve of his smile turns immediately to an upside-down frown.

"Ptooey!" He spits a piece of gum at her, but she dodges aside. If she had not, it would have gone in her hair, just like the unhappy unbirthday party a few months ago, when some one had spit a piece of gum in the back of her head. When she'd turned around they'd all denied it, laughing. She'd always suspected it had been Humpty.

But she has more pressing matters to attend to rather than bringing that up again.

He shakes his fist at her while scowling. "Why you little brat! I should spank you! Get onto my lap and take your punishment!"

He only wants me to go up there because he won't come down here. He only ever leaves that wall to attend my unhappy unbirthday parties.

She shouts, "Only if you give my heart back!" She isn't sure he took it, because the Tweedles might have lied about it, but perhaps she can trick him into confessing.

He chuckles, smiling big again. "Why, my dear brat, I haven't got it on me. Can't you see?" He spreads wide his arms. "You know everything I have I either carry with me or set against my wall…"

It's true. Humpty requires few possessions. Indeed, he *can't* have too many because he spends all his time on his wall and can only carry so much on him. He also sets a few possessions at the base of his wall, but those possessions are very few indeed. But she can't see the other side of the wall right now…

Again, Alice tries pretending to know more than she actually does. "But I saw you take it!"

"Did you now? Well, if I did, maybe I gave it away!"

"To who?"

"To *whom*. Mind your grammar."

"To whom?"

"None of your business."

Alice scowls and puts one arm akimbo. "It certainly *is* my business! It was *my* heart!"

"Finders keepers."

"You didn't find it. You stole it."

"You seem to be doing fine without it. Why it's like an appendix! Completely unnecessary!"

She narrows her eyes. "Do you have one?"

"An appendix? Of course not. I'm not a book!"

"No, a heart."

"Your heart? No, I told you already."

She argghs in frustration. "No, a heart inside you."

"What do you think?"

She thinks maybe he doesn't have a heart at all—maybe none of the citizens of Wonderland do—*that's what makes them so vicious. And now that I'm like them, I can use that to my advantage.*

She says, "How do I know you're not lying about my heart? Maybe it's around here somewhere." She peers around and starts to circle the little wall. It's indeed little, barely wide enough to fit Humpty's bottom. It's a wall that blocks or guards nothing at all.

As she walks, he mockingly laughs at her. He laughs so hard that his huge saucer eyes begin to tear up.

"Look all you want, little girl! Why would I even bother lying to you! Why, you wouldn't do anything about it no matter what I do. You wouldn't hurt a fly!" He's mocking her, reminding her of the prank he had played on her—with the meat and flies.

Her eyes go wide as on the other side of the wall, she sees the roll of tape resting at the base—the tape he uses to bind her wrists while tormenting her.

"Ah, so you remember the tape? Why it's only one of the two world possessions I need. I only need toys to play with you with. I have no use for your heart! But perhaps if you're good and play with me, I'll help you get it back."

She shoots hatred at him with her eyes. "Why would you want that?" Meanwhile, she's thinking, He *mentioned another possession but I don't see it anywhere...*

He says, "Those with hearts suffer more. More fun to play with. And I must say, ever since you've lost yours, you seem much more disobedient. In need of some punishment. Oh, how I love to punish you!"

At this point, Alice has circled back around where she began, facing up at the egg-shaped man sitting atop his perch.

She says, defiantly, "Now that I have no heart, perhaps you should be afraid. I might strike back now, be ruthless."

"Poppycock, brat! I'm still stronger than you and the weak succumb to the mighty." And here he raises his arms in the air like a victorious gladiator—and a glint of metal flashes in his hand—she focuses her eyes and realizes it's the razorblade.

"Yes!" he says. "This is the second possession. It is the very same one. The same one I cut you with at your unhappy unbirthday party, do you remember?"

"I remember. I had the sniffles, so you offered to help me by bleeding me. That was kind of you. It cured me. It made me think perhaps you weren't so bad."

He laughs. "You idiot! Bloodletting doesn't do anything for a cold. I tricked you! Are you really so dense? You willingly let me slice you! All the other fellows and I had a great laugh at that behind your back. We were just waiting for the perfect moment to reveal it to you. It's all about timing don't you know."

Her face shows shock and outrage, but before she realizes and tries to hide it, it's already too late—he's seen.

He laughs at her. "A priceless expression. Worthy of a portrait. So what are you going to do, now that you're heartless? Are you thinking you'll topple me? Is that it?" He quickly slices the blade through the air then calls out:

"I'm Humpty Dumpty, here on my wall!
I'm Humpty Dumpty, and I cannot fall!
I'll kick you and slice you and kill you and more!
And when it all ends, you'll be covered in gore!"

Alice feels such hatred come over her towards him—she had felt it before, when she had a heart, but she had never acted on it—because she couldn't bring herself to harm another. It was much nobler, she had felt, to suffer in humility. She felt she would be rewarded in the end, for there was the saying—the meek shall inherit the earth. And she had been as meek as she could possibly manage. And she used to try to be so trusting of others.

But now that she is heartless, she is much less naive and she almost expects everyone to be deceitful, for she now realizes there is so much advantage in it. Why should she believe a word this egghead says? Perhaps he had grown curious and taken the heart as his own. She wouldn't put it past him. She wouldn't put anything past anyone. And she now marvels at her old self—*how could I have been so naive before, thinking perhaps everyone had good motives, that everyone has a good side to them, even though it may perhaps be buried deep. When the truth is there is much to be gained from being heartless, immoral.*

She says to him, "You know, when I asked if you had a heart inside you, you asked, 'What do you think?' You never said no."

He waves his razorblade brandishing hand. "Technicalities. Pish posh. Haberdash."

"So I'll tell you what I think. I think I don't know what to think. I know you say you're not an egg, but you sure look like an egg. And whatever you are, you could certainly fit a lot of things inside you. And just a short while ago, the Tweedles recited to me a most curious poem. About when one of them broke you open. Do you know it?"

The egg-shaped man grimaces. "That I do."

"There is a particular couplet I find most intriguing. Do you know the one?"

He grins ferociously. "Why don't you tell me, earless girl." He points with the razorblade.

With a fright, she lifts her hands to her ears, feels them still there. She scowls at him, sure her face must be scrunching up severely.

Humpty says, "Sorry. Just practicing calling you that. You were speaking of the poem."

She nods, lowers her hands that form fists. "'If you just rush, and don't stop for a minute, you'll end up with too much of your *own* self within it.' They wouldn't explain. It seems to imply that if someone like me broke you open and tried to cook the insides, I'd 'put too much of my own self in it.' It might be a play on words, or perhaps you literally have a part of myself inside you. Like my heart." She glares at him suspiciously.

He glares at her. "Is that what you think?"

She decides to taunt him, before her next planned move, which is to topple him. It looks like it would barely take a nudge. "Which one pushed you over? Tweedle dee or dum? It only took one? Did the other sit and watch and laugh and point?"

Indignantly, "Why, the other one wasn't there yet!"

Alice fights to keep from grinning. She had tricked him into revealing more than he had intended. She could get used to this being deceptive without a heart thing. *But no! I have to get my heart back! I mustn't lose sight of that fact, even if I start forgetting the reasons why…*

She looks at him in a pitying expression, "And yet, still, it only took one? Is it because you're egg shaped?"

"He just caught me off guard is all! But that was a long time ago. I've been practicing my balance. It would take a hurricane to knock me off now. A hurricane! And you, little girl, though you blow hot air, are not one." And he crosses his arms.

Alice decides to lie again, just to see if she can tease more information out of him. "So they said, that after they both broke you, they made a scrumptious omelet. Bacon, cheese, and ham! Yummy!"

His cheeks flare red. *Why if he were an egg, he might be hard boiling himself right now,* she thinks with a giggle.

"Lies! I cannot stand a liar! I hope those two *do* end up killing each other over that rattle!" He crosses his arms, harumphs.

"Oh I bet you can't name one lie in what they said. I think they're quite honest."

He scooches his head slightly to the side, disdainful. "First of all, I am not an egg! So they made no omelet! That's a bald faced lie! And second, it wasn't the both of them that broke me. Why the other one had not even been born yet!"

"What do you mean, not born yet?

He clamps his mouth. "You ask too many questions!"

"So it only took one of them to topple you!" Mocking laugh.

"It's not like that! I was caught off guard from my usual superb balance. There was a snake."

"A snake?"

"Yes, I'm deathly afraid of snakes. Snakes like to eat eggs you see, even though I'm not one. An egg, that is. The snake gave me such a fright that I lost my superb balance a bit, and Tweedledee nudged me over, and well, I had a great fall."

"Boom! Crash!" She jumps to add drama, making clawing hands.

Humpty Dumpty leans back in surprise, teetering a little, but doesn't quite completely lose balance.

She sneers. "So did you land sunnyside up?"

"I tell you I'm not an egg!"

"So what was inside?"

"You've irritated me so much, now I won't tell."

She peers at him. "It seems maybe you could store things inside, to hide things away."

"We all hide things away."

"So what *is* inside you?"

"You want to know what's inside? I'll tell you:

Oh, I am just like you within,
Just like a heartless Alice.
Just like your dark and hateful twin,
Who's brought to birth by malice.

That dark and hateful twin who shows
Inside the glass reflection.
Who with time only *stronger* grows,
From all your imperfection.

We all have that dark twin of us,
Who gazes from the mirror,
Who threatens to replace us,
As darkness edges nearer.

'Where's my old self?' one day you'll say,
As you gaze into the glass.
The dark twin now is here to stay,
And your old self's gone and past.

Maybe he's hiding my heart inside him, maybe he's not. Either way, he deserves to die.

She charges him—as she runs, the rattle sounds—she slams her palm under Humpty's mouth. As she pushes with all her might, the rattle sounds again.

Humpty sways backward precariously but doesn't fall—he slashes out with the razorblade and Alice instinctively jumps back.

Humpty is looking around with worried eyes. "What was that sound? Did you hear it?"

Alice doesn't know what he's talking about. Now she feels the trickle of liquid rolling down her cheek. She touches her face. She sees red blood on her fingertips. She won't know how bad she's cut until she can get to a mirror.

Humpty's glaring at her. "You've got a little boo boo." He licks the side of the razorblade.

Alice doesn't want to risk any more injury. *If I leave him there, he won't follow me. He never leaves that wall except for my unhappy unbirthday parties, but I'll have to worry about that later.*

Now something nags at the back of her brain. The rattle. Could it be he'd thought it was a snake?

She gasps and points at the base of the wall. "What was that? I thought I saw a rattlesnake!" She hopes her acting is convincing enough.

In a shrill voice he says, "What, a snake? You lie! Where?"

Alice approaches the wall with a look of grave concern, with her hand crinkled against her mouth. "I—I think it slithered to the other side, behind you!"

"What?"

Alice watches Humpty's eyes. He turns slightly to look and when he's no longer watching her, she reaches into her dress pocket and gives the rattle a jostle.

Humpty shrieks, panic on his face. He quickly turns to face Alice, begins swiveling, looking around. "Where is it? Kill it!"

"There!" She points to her left, where he's not looking. As he turns to look he seems very careless in his balance and teeters quite dangerously.

While he's looking she runs to the other side of the wall and shakes the rattle.

"Eeek!" he shrieks and lurches around to look, wobbles precariously and almost topples forward. He barely saves himself by windmilling his arms.

Alice briefly considers pulling him forward to topple him but she still fears getting cut.

She shrieks, points. "There behind you!" She doesn't explain how unlikely it would be for a snake to be floating in midair, which is where she is pointing.

Humpty roars while twirling, lashing out with his blade. He's quite off balance now, he almost fell just then.

And now Alice roars as she shoves him with both hands and he screams as he falls off. She hears a cracking crunch sound from the other side of the wall, then the sound of eggshell parts settling.

She proclaims:

"Humpty Dumpty sat on a wall.

Humpty Dumpty said, "I can't fall!"

But he got so afraid from just a toy's sound,

That he lost his safe seat, and slammed into the ground!"

MaLiCe

She rushes to look. She sees no yolk or egg white, though she sees many bits of broken egg shells on the ground, and here and there are different parts of Humpty's facial features. And she sees a young girl, partially covered in egg shell bits. The girl's in an odd position—she's upside down balancing on the back of her neck, her body bent with her legs flung over and bent so that her feet rest on the ground.

Alice gasps. "Oh, dear! Are you okay?"

"I don't know. It's kind of hard to tell in this odd position. Are you gonna just stand there?" She wiggles her hand a little bit.

"Oh, I'm sorry! Where are my manners?" Alice helps the girl right herself.

The girl sits on the ground amongst the debris, patting eggshells off herself. The girl looks just like Alice!

Alice shouts, "Why you look just like me!"

"Do I?"

"Why yes, with the very same clothing! And…" Here she points at the clean straight slash upon the girl's left cheek, which had left a small streak of blood. "You have a cut on your cheek, just like me! Only yours is on your left cheek!"

The girl lifts her hand up to her cheek and gasps when she sees the blood on her fingers.

Alice notices that the girl uses her right hand, so she asks, "Are you right handed? I'm left."

The girl says, "Well, I suppose I am, right handed that is."

"Why it's like you're the mirror image of me! I'm Alice. What's your name?"

"I am…" She ponders for a moment, her eyes moving to gaze upward. Her mouth switches between rising on one side then the other. Alice recognizes it as something she does herself. The girl says, "I don't know!"

"Where did you come from? Do you remember being inside the egg?"

"I don't know, and no!"

Alice asks, "Remember being cut with a razorblade?"

"No, I remember nothing! All I know is the past few moments."

"Oh, dear. Well you're the only person I know who was born from out an egg! But, first thing first, you need a name I should think, so we can be told apart!"

"Okay," says the girl. "I want your name."

Alice tries to take on a patient tone, as if she were lecturing someone. "Oh no, I had it first. But…I have an idea. You came from an egg-shaped man who claimed not to be an egg. But that's beside the point. He recited a poem to me before he fell. His poem spoke of a twin 'brought to birth by malice'. I'm not quite sure if you have much malice, but it rhymes with Alice in any case and seems a fine name to me! What do you say? Do you like it?"

"Yes," says the girl with a smile that Alice finds both alluring and creepy at the same time, "that suits me just fine."

Alice helps Malice to stand.

During the next moments, they talk and Alice gathers the tape, razorblade and rattle up and puts the items in her pockets. Alice does her best to explain things to Malice in a brief manner. Alice is sure she must have forgotten to mention at least one important detail, but she wants to continue with her mission to regain her heart. She has no intention whatsoever of trying to put Humpty Dumpty together again, because the guy was a sadist and she's glad he's broken, even though the old Alice with a heart might have felt much guilt.

When the subject turns to hearts, it's soon found that Malice is heartless as well, for none beats in her chest.

"Oh dear," says Alice. "Why, whenever we *do* regain my heart, there will be only one of them between us! Perhaps if we shared?"

But Malice waves that off. "Let's not worry about that right now. Besides, from what you told me, having a heart seems like such a burden. I would think it might be better to go without one!"

Alice doesn't have a good answer to that, because she feels the same, but the fact of the matter is that some of her property has been stolen from her, and she can not abide the insult. She will do whatever is necessary to recover her rightful property. And who knows, maybe afterwards, she'll realize how great having a heart can be.

"Come," Alice says, "Let us now go back to the Tweedles. I'm hoping by now, one has killed the other. If they're still alive, though, don't give them too much information. And for that matter, don't let *any*one know that we're heartless, for we can use their ignorance to our advantage. I realize that now."

A few minutes later, they stop walking as they see, appearing above the ground in front of them, a feline grin.

Alice says, "It's the Cheshire Cat. Watch, and soon his head will appear."

Moments later, the cat's eyes appear, then the rest of his head. To Alice, he says, "Not only are you not dead, but you've doubled since before."

Alice says, "I'm so sorry. It's just that I haven't had time to kill myself. It's just that I have odds and ends to take care of, you see."

"Well, I can be patient, but I can't wait all my last life!" He chuckles, now he shifts attention to Malice. "Greetings. Who might you be?"

"Malice." She looks confused for a moment before curtseying with her black dress.

The cat says, "Well you two are like mirror images of each other." He speaks even as he grins that huge grin of his. "Twice the fun. Imagine. A double suicide! Wonderland's first!"

Malice opens her mouth to speak, but Alice cuts her off, saying, "Yes, Malice wants to kill herself too. In fact we've signed a suicide pact. It'll be very soon and you can watch!"

The cat says, "Yessss…I want to watch. Will you cry first? Yummy yummy." He licks his lips. Everyone thinks Alice's tears are magical and delicious, but she wonders if that's still true now that she's heartless.

Alice uses a cooing, purring. "Yes, we'll cry our delicious tears. We'll even let you lick them, because you're going to help us both escape this horrible world."

"Yessss." The cat purrs. "Lick your sweet innocent faces, taste the tears of your sweet sorrow mmmm."

Alice cocks her head to the side flirtatiously. "Yes, there's only one problem, though. The gun you gave me only has one shot. It's a dueling pistol. We need another one if we're going to both blow our brains out."

"Yesss, yesss. I see. And you both promise to kill yourselves and let me watch? Soon?" His voice sounds whiny, pouty.

Everyone in Wonderland knows that Alice would rather die than break a promise. That was the old Alice with a heart, though. But so long as he didn't know that she and Malice were heartless, she'd use the deception to her advantage.

Alice says, "I pwomise." Ending with a cutesy pout. She looks over at Malice.

"And I pwomise too, Mister Cat!" She places her finger to the edge of her mouth then shifts her eyes to look upward and to the side.

The cat says, "Okay, just so long as you don't go shooting yourselves without me. But the most I can manage is the other dueling pistol in the set. These things don't grow on trees you know. So don't become triplets. Hold on while I fetch it, and I must insist that afterward you refrain from speaking, as I have a lunch date I must attend to. Hold on…" and the cat begins to disappear, in this order: outside, then eyes, then mouth, then reappears in the opposite order, but this time, his grinning mouth holds an ivory handled pistol. When his head again fully appears, (He, as usual, neglects his body.) He gives the pistol to Malice

"Sorry," he says, "no time to waste. Remember, no shooting without me, my doppletwinners! But I must go capture lunch!" He begins to disappear.

Alice sees this as a wonderful opportunity to shout the cat a question by surprise before he has time to think. She must hurry, because if she shouts after his ears disappear he won't hear her. She shouts, "Just curious. If one of us became heartless, how would our tears taste?"

The outer edge of the cat's head vanishes, but his mouth says, "Why they'd taste like burning because they'd be acid! Why do you—" But now he's disappeared.

What Alice had suspected is true, it seems.

Malice is testing the heft of the pistol. "Instead of killing ourselves, why don't we kill that stupid cat? Pow! Right between the eyes! I wonder if he'll stop grinning before he dies."

Alice smiles at the thought but then shakes her head. "He'd probably just disappear before we could shoot him. The Queen of Hearts keeps trying to kill him. She's succeeded several times already. But that's why, now, he only shows his head, because if he has no body, he can't be beheaded."

Malice says, "Well that's a shame. So what are we to do with this pistol?"

"You haven't met the Tweedles yet. I have an idea. Just follow my lead, okay?"

"You got it, twin!"

ReTurn to the TweEdles

Soon, they arrive at the the Tweedles' tree.

Alice curses silently to herself as she sees that the two brothers are still alive, circling around the pistol on the ground, glaring at each other.

"Mine!" says Tweedledee.

"Contrariwise!" shouts the other.

They are so engrossed in their spat that they fail to notice Alice and Malice.

How can they not see us? Alice thinks. *What a bunch of morons. If they can't help me get my heart back, then they will both die for what they did to me. Good thing I have Malice as my backup.*

She motions Malice over, and together they sneak into position. They stand and wait for the Tweedles to circle around. Malice takes out her pistol, and Alice lifts her chain. She's worried that hitting a Tweedle with it might not do enough harm, though. When they are each behind one of the Tweedles, Alice nods.

Alice's chain makes a clinky sound as she shifts it, about to strike.

With seemingly impossible speed, the Tweedles both twirl and kick. Alice is knocked to the ground, dazed. She struggles to recover but within moments she is being sat upon by Tweedledee. She looks over to see that Malice is held down as well.

Tweedledee rummages through her pockets and empties the contents onto the ground. He says, "Aha! Humpty's tape!" He tapes Alice's arms behind her back before tossing the tape to his brother, who tapes Malice up. The Tweedle twins get off of them, then pull them up so they're sitting on the ground.

Tweedledum proclaims, "Why there are two of you now, just like us!"

"Contrariwise!" Tweedledee shouts. "They're not like us! They're taped up!"

"That's not what I meant," Tweedledum says. He wiggles the pistol in his hand. "Why I oughta shoot you dead right now!"

"No way, no how! That's an unfair contest! Foul!" Tweedledee shakes the rattle viciously at his brother.

"No how back! You can't call a foul, if I haven't done the thing yet. Forfeit!"

Now Alice decides to cut in, while trying to put some of her newfound art of deception into good use. "Boys, boys, the gun is not real. It's merely a cap gun. A toy!"

They look down at her.

Tweedledee holds the razorblade underneath Alice's chin, pressed against the skin. "But this razorblade is real, I can tell. I think it would be a good tool for making you cry. What do you think brother?"

"Ditto. Twice the eyes, twice the tears. Delicious!" He rubs his tummy.

"Ditto to your ditto." Tweedledee addresses Alice now. "So since there are two of you, we take it you cracked open Humpty? Excellent. We always hated that blowhard."

"Yes," Alice says. "We had a bit of a break up."

Tweedledee says, "Excellent! But we have a bit of a confession. Humpty didn't have your heart."

"I know that now."

Tweedledum says, "Yes, we thought it would be grand fun to have you go after Humpty. But the truth is that after he took your heart at the party, in exchange for a future favor, he handed it off to the Mad Hatter, who snuck it out under his hat."

Tweedledee says, "Yes, we played a bit of a practical joke on you. And now there are two of you! And we shall have twice as much fun making you cry!"

Alice knows that she and Malice are not in a good position to stop them, but she has an idea. "But before that, I have an idea! A way for you to settle your differences and decide who shall have the rattle!"

"I have the rattle!" Tweedledee proclaims, and to prove it, he gives it a little shake.

Alice says, "Well I have a nice idea, regardless. It'll be a fun game. Since you two are always feuding and dueling…"

"Yes?" the brothers both say at the same time. They are leaning forward on tippy toes, in anticipation.

Alice says, "Why not have a duel? A pretend duel? Why it will be fun. And then you can both pretend to die. Isn't it such grand fun to pretend to be shot?"

The Tweedles are nodding eagerly with big grins on their faces as they say, "Ditto!"

One of them even gives a preview of his performance, clutching his chest, and sticking his tongue out the side of his mouth.

But, "Not yet!" Malice scolds.

Alice looks over at Malice who is grinning huge before she nods, now letting Alice do all the talking.

Alice says, "Malice and I can judge who dies the best, and the winner, hrmmm…" She pretends to think. "What shall the prize be?"

Now the brothers put their hands to their chins, repeating, "Prize prize prize." And they seem to be thinking hard.

Alice knows that anything they come up with will only lead to another round of arguing. So Alice jumps in, saying, "First one to lick our tears?"

The brothers consider that a moment, then nod. "Ditto!" they proclaim.

Each of the brothers grabs a pistol and soon they are standing back to back.

Tweedledum says, "Can we get on with this, please?"

"Yes, of course," Alice says. "Now, no pussyfooting you two. You have to actually aim and everything. You must convince us of your performance! And no cheating. You don't fire until I say. Now, as I count you shall take your steps until 20, then turn when I say fire."

One of them says "Nohow" while the other says "Contrariwise," then the both of them: "Too far!"

"Fine then, 19 steps."

"18!" Tweedledee shouts, while the other shouts, "2!" Alice says, "10."

"17!" Tweedledee shouts, while the other shouts, "5!"

Alice says, "At this rate, we'll never agree! I say 3, and that's final! Now…" She begins to count to three—like mirror images of each other, the twins take their steps, then Alice shouts, "Fire!"

They turn at the same time, lift their pistols at the same rate and fire simultaneously. Blooms of red sprout in identical areas of their chests and they each raise a hand to their chests, drop their pistols at the same time.

Malice shouts, "Yay!" She claps a little with her bound hands.

The Tweedles' hands clutched to their chests are growing red with blood, the red on their shirts growing wider.

Tweedledum shouts, "Real bullets, I daresay!" He groans in pain.

Tweedledee says, "Ditto! Shot through our hearts we are!" in a sorrowful tone.

They stagger at the same time.

Like looking at mirror images, Alice thinks.

Malice is mocking them, "Ahah! A couple of buffoons. I rename you DumDum and DumDummerer!"

Their faces flash anger before returning to their pained expressions.

Tweedledee glances at the razorblade he had set down. "Revenge I daresay, is warranted brother. Let's cut their throats!"

"Contrariwise! Let's shoot them with the guns."

"Splendid thinking brother! Ditto!"

The brothers take their bloodied hands from off their chests to stoop and pick up the guns.

Malice's expression takes on a look of fear.

Alice doesn't know much about guns, but could it be possible that the Cheshire Cat had lied about them being single shot?

The Tweedle twins begin staggering toward their targets. Every once in a while they must stop and shout in pain, and their hands tremble, but they make their way.

Malice shouts, "No! Back off! Go away!"

Alice sneers, says to Tweedledee. "I'm surprised. I guess you have hearts after all."

He answers, "Yes, but they're black."

Alice says nothing. Merely locks eyes with Tweedledee as he approaches—she doesn't move her eyes from his, holds a cold unblinking stare. He had been responsible for so much torment and she had taken it, but now, she's determined to stare into his eyes as the life leaves him. She wants to see the very moment he dies.

Closer he comes.

Tweedledee stands before Alice. Tweedledum is in front of Malice. As one, the twins lift the pistols, never breaking eye contact with the girl in front of them. They point the pistols at the girls' forehead and pull the triggers.

And the pistols go *click*.

"No boom boom," Alice says with a glare, looking into his eyes, and then, as she'd hoped, she sees the life leave him, as his eyeballs roll up into his head, and he topples over on top of her, causing her to be pushed over and having her cheek pressed into the dirt.

She hears Malice screaming, "Ahhh! Get this fat whale off of me!"

It takes a few moments for Alice to wiggle out from under the corpse. Malice is already free. The boys seemed to have died at the same time, like twins to the very end.

As Alice struggles to free herself, she watches as Malice goes over to the razorblade and awkwardly uses it to cut at her tape bonds. Alice offers to help, but for some reason, Malice absolutely refuses. Malice's efforts are awkward but seem to be working. Meanwhile, Alice gets out from under the dead body.

Alice feels a sharp pain in her wrist and yells out. Malice yells out at the same time.

Malice shouts, "I cut myself!"

Alice's hands are behind her, so she doesn't know what the cause of *her* pain was.

Her hands growing bloody from her wound, Malice continues to saw away. She pulls her hands apart, the tape finally cut away.

Malice approaches Alice with a wicked grin on her face. "And now, to take care of you."

Alice says, "Thank you so much. I need to get some circulation back." She chuckles, glad to have her helper and teammate on her side, to help her get her heart back.

Malice crouches down behind her. "What is this? You have a slice on your wrist too? How did that happen?"

"I don't know, it was at the same time as you cut yourself." Alice feels her hair pulled violently back and held there, feels the razorblade pressed to her neck.

From behind, Malice whispers in her ear, "Don't move and this will go quickly. Don't speak. I remember what you told me. The problem is, there is only one heart between the two of us. One of us must go."

"If you cut me, you cut yourself!"

"What?" The pressure of the blade lessens slightly.

"My wrist! Your cheek! We're mirror images. If I die, you die!"

There is a long pause, then the blade leaves Alice's neck.

Quietly, Malice says, "Damn." She raises her voice to address Alice, but remains behind her, out of sight.

"Well that certainly complicates things. So I suppose you are my rival. Good luck to you. But remember, finders keepers."

"It doesn't have to be like that. Maybe we can share somehow. This is Wonderland after all. We can still work together. Getting back my...I mean *our* heart is the most important thing. Then we can compromise." She waits for a response. "Just release me, okay?"

No response. Malice is gone.

Alice is able to stand, and looks around. Malice has taken the razorblade and chains and one pistol. The other pistol remains, but it's useless and heavy. Her dress pockets may be able to hold a lot, but holding too much would get clunky and heavy. The tape remains, which Alice awkwardly slips into her dress, and thankfully she still has her deck of cards. When she gets her hands free she'll have to look through it to see if the Thirteen of Heartless is still in there, but she suspects it is, because she realizes she forgot to tell Malice that she'd need the card in order to put the heart back in.

And of course, the two corpses of the Tweedles remain, lying in the blood-soaked dirt. The rattle is lying on the ground a few feet away from them, forgotten.

She says, "Who wants the rattle, then?" She looks over at Tweedledum, who is lying face down in the dirt. "You? Hey, look at me when I'm talking to you. Fine then." She walks to the rattle and after struggling a bit, picks it up, carries it over to Tweedledee, who is lying face up, and tosses it onto his chest. "There, now you have your precious rattle. Ga ga goo goo, you little baby." She stares at his unmoving face, frozen in a contorted expression of pain. "Where's my thank you? Well fine, guess I'll go."

After a few moments thought, she decides to visit the Caterpillar, who lives a short distance away, to get untaped. She begins walking.

After a few moments, she stops, turns to look at you, and recites this poem:

Tweedledum and Tweedledee,
Were each given a fake toy gun,
So that Tweedledum and Tweedledee,
Could pretend duel and die just for fun.

So they tried to see who best could act,
As if they were shot by a gun,
But real shots rang out, and their ribs both were cracked,
And they died without saying who won!

The Caterpillar

Soon she comes to it, a spot to the side of the path where there is a particular mushroom atop which sits a particular three inch long caterpillar smoking from a hookah.

She awkwardly positions herself to take a tiny bite of the mushroom, as the little caterpillar watches tinily and quietly.

She was required to visit the caterpillar every other day, but that was before her heart got stolen. Biting from the left side of the mushroom always makes her shrink.

And shrink she does. Just as she suspected, everything shrinks at a different rate—her clothes always shrink a bit slower than her body, causing her dress to temporarily be too big for her, and what she was counting on is also true—her arms and wrists shrink faster than the tape wrapped around them, so soon she is easily able to pull her hands free.

She sits now, on the ground, a respectable size for conversing with the atrocious insect. She doesn't like him at all. He's immature, literally—he refuses to grow up and become a butterfly. But she'd always been too polite to protest with any more than a level of meekly.

The Caterpillar watches her with detached interest from his differently spectacled eyes—a year ago, he took to wearing a monocle on one eye to appear more distinguished. He lifts the hookah from his insectoid mouth and shoots smoke rings in her direction. "You snuck up on me! Usually I have to put up with your distracting shadow over me before you shrink. Why I say girl! Do you know you're not casting a shadow?"

Alice looks down to see that it's true. But she shrugs it off. Weird things happen all the time in Wonderland.

Alice brings out her deck of cards and begins looking through it, quickly finding that the Thirteen of Heartless is still there.

Now the Caterpillar says, "Cards? What's the meaning, girl? And why did you put tape around your wrists?"

Alice is grateful for the freedom to fold her arms, which she does now. "I didn't do it. It was the Tweedle twins. They—they were trying to make me cry." Since she had so recently acquired the skill of deception, she decides to put it to use now, and pretend she's the same

Alice as usual—and she won't mention the twins' demise.

The Caterpillar takes a small puff from his hookah, exhales smoke. "Boys will be boys."

"Brats will be brats. They will get what's coming to them someday."

"Perhaps, but not from the likes of you. Why, you are just a weak, little...meek, uninspiring, unimpressive, tiny little little girl."

"You should be glad I am. That way, I can talk to you."

"Yes, I'm glad to make you test for me, but I know you. You would goof off if you could. Won't stay on task. You're lucky to have me to provide you with guidance." He tuts and adjusts his monocle with one of his many many thin caterpillar legs.

Alice tries to stifle her anger. Her goal here is not to give in to her anger, despite all the horrible things the Caterpillar has done to her in the past. Her goal is to get to the bottom of where her heart is. *I must keep reminding myself of that.*

Alice says, "I'm grateful for your tutelage. You've taught me so much of the effects of so many varied spices. Why, recount with me—spices that have made my hair turned red, spices that have made all the food I ate taste like strawberries and one that made me feel dizzy as if I'd been spinning in place for minutes at a time. And one that shot me full of so much pleasure I lay still for three days straight. Once you gave me a spice that made rainbows shoot from my mouth each time I spoke. Do you remember?"

He chuckles. "Yes, I remember that one. You are lucky to know someone with such a refined taste and such access to numerous spices as I have. Do you realize how exquisite of a hookah smoker I am?"

Alice fights to keep from rolling her eyes. *How can I forget? You mention it every single time.* But she thinks perhaps it's wise to stroke his ego a bit before she tries to tease any information out of him. So she says, "How exquisite?"

"Glad you asked! Why my girl, I am so skilled a hookaher, that no matter the spice, no matter if I have ever smoked it or not, I can inhale precisely and exactly up to the very moment just before an overdose would occur. It is a simply uncanny skill I have and a testament to my skills and abilities. And so I am able to reach the pinnacle of pleasure that each spice offers, for it is right on that line just before you get too much that you get the most you can get without getting too much, you see?"

Alice nods eagerly. Even while, for so long, and right now even, she has wished that the Caterpillar would make a mistake some day and inhale just a little too long and die and be rid of himself. Because frankly, she doesn't appreciate being the test subject for his tinkering.

Now the Caterpillar adjusts his monocle and launches into his favorite poem, which he recites often, and which so happens to be about himself.

I'm an insect hookaher of distinction and taste,
Who smokes the most exquisite spices!
And I know when to quit with the utmost of haste,
So as not to be killed by my vices!

Since I inhale right up to the point that I die,
I reach the highest point of pleasure,
And since my timing's so precise, so clever am I,
Why I daresay that I am a treasure!

Alice claps at his recitation. She's quite convincing, she thinks.

"Very good, my girl. Thank you for your support. I have a new spice for you..."

The Caterpillar likes to test all his newly acquired spices on her. He calls her his "guinea pig". It has resulted in so much misery and recoveries over the years, she has grown to despise him. Yet she could never refuse him, because he threatened to tell the Queen, who would order guards to have her beaten or whipped if she made trouble.

She says, meekly, "I'd rather not try it. More for you, don't you think?"

"Oh, no, my little girl. I'm unfamiliar with this particular spice. I need you to test it so I can watch you and know how much to take without overdosing. You know that. Must we go through this again?"

Alice sighs. So many times she's wished the Caterpillar *would* overdose so he wouldn't be able to torment her anymore. She'd fantasized about maybe "helping" him get a little too much over the edge, but she could never before bring herself to do it. But she has more things to worry about than revenge, she reminds herself.

"Okay," she says smiling. "But before I toke, there's something I'd like to discuss."

He adjusts his monocle, blows some smoke. "Yes?"

"See, during my unhappy unbirthday party today…I know you weren't there, but perhaps you might have heard something. I had something stolen. A very important item. Have you heard anything about it?"

"I've heard nothing, and why should I care? What was stolen? Don't you take care of your possessions, silly girl?"

"Well it's quite embarrassing. I'll just say it was a body part. Are you sure you've heard nothing? You don't happen to know where it might be, do you?"

"A body part? What body part?" He looks around theatrically. "Well it's certainly not around here. Why, depending on which part, it would probably be quite huge compared to me. Have you not forgotten that you're usually overly large? And your *body parts* would be overly large?" His tone of speaking suggests he thinks Alice is stupid.

"And you don't happen to know—"

He waves four arms, dismissively. "No no, no one tells me anything. They consider me too *tiny* to speak to. When really it is *they* who are overly large! Now enough of your missing property. You look just fine to me! I'm so anxious to try my new spice. Now get up here girl! You wouldn't want me to tell the Queen would you?"

Alice believes the Caterpillar knows nothing about her lost heart. If the Tweedle twins hadn't been lying, the Mad Hatter had taken it, so he's next on her list to visit.

The Caterpillar causes her to startle from her thoughts when he shouts, "Girl! Get up here, get up here now! I'll tell the Queen if you don't come this instant! I shall have you whipped, beaten, beheaded! A trivial missing body part will be the least of your worries when you're missing your head! Now!" His face has grown crimson from rage and his monocle drops carelessly from his eye and swings from the angry jerking motions of his head.

A grin creeps up Alice's face as she locks eyes with him. "Certainly." She curtsies.

Come, we shall have some fun now. And perhaps when I toke, the high of the spice will be a jolly good time besides. I always felt such guilt at the pleasure before, but that was the old me.

The Caterpillar says, "I'm glad to see some obedience for a change." As Alice begins to climb the mushroom, he says, "That's a good girl." Now that she's on top of it, he says, "Come sit in my lap."

The Caterpillar doesn't actually have a lap in the human sense, but Alice snuggles in front of the Caterpillar, huggled by dozens of his waving arms.

The Caterpillar begins to put the spice into his hookah. The spice looks like dried green leaves. "Now this spice," the Caterpillar says, "is supposed to cause imaginations in the mind, colors and tastes to fill your head. It's quite powerful." The new spice begins to burn. "Here now." He holds the mouthpiece part up to her lips. "Just like always, with the two breaths."

The usual routine is for Alice to take two tokes while the Caterpillar watches. He has an uncanny ability to judge how powerful any spice is just by watching, so that he knows exactly how long to inhale himself, right up to the exact moment before an overdose—that way, he can achieve the highest high possible.

Eagerly, Alice takes the mouthpiece into her mouth, inhales warm rough smoke, fills her lungs, does it again. She coughs up smoke. Now she feels a tingling in her head and a sensation as if her head is expanding.

"Ooh, I can't wait," the Caterpillar says. His voice sounds deeper than usual, and slower. He takes the pipe from her hand, lifts it to his mouth, and inhales.

Alice acts as quickly as she can, though she's a little clumsy from the spice. She grabs the tape from her pocket. The Caterpillar is inhaling deeply, eyes closed, not noticing her.

Alice peels the tape, sticks one end to the back of the Caterpillar's head then wraps the tape around, taping the hookah in place in the Caterpillar's mouth.

The Caterpillar still has his eyes closed. Perhaps the spice has numbed his sense of touch.

Alice makes sure to tape over the Caterpillar's nose holes.

She shouts, "Take that!"

The Caterpillar is slow to react, but his eyes dreamily open. He seems confused as he sees Alice staring deeply into his eyes. He looks around, then his eyes go wide in surprise as he realizes.

"Do you know what body part I lost?" Alice says as the Caterpillar tries to rip the tape off, but his arms are too weak and caterpillary. "My heart." The whites of the Caterpillar's eyes show quite a bit more as he glances at her. She glares back, and takes the tube in her hand, because she figures that's what he'll try next.

And he does—he tries to pull the tubing from the hookah. Alice slaps his hands away with her free hand. It's easy to do, because his movements are clumsy and slow.

The Caterpillar yells a muffled scream of rage and terror from behind the tape. Alice figures the Caterpillar had been holding his breath, so screaming would lead to...

The Caterpillar takes a deep breath. He blinks and shakes his head, his eyes go wide, he begins to twitch.

Alice watches.

The Caterpillar begins to shake all over. His eyes roll up into the top of his head. He lurches to the side and drops off the mushroom, and Alice is yanked and falls too, because she is too clumsy from the spice.

The Caterpillar thuds heavily onto the ground on his backside. Alice lands on top of him. She hears the hookah land somewhere to her left.

She feels groggy and dazed and for a few long seconds, they lie that way. She feels the Caterpillar's chest rise as he takes in another deep breath.

Several long seconds pass. Alice looks around, trying to plan her mode of getting off the bastard. Should she just roll off and trust she'll land okay?

But now the Caterpillar's body starts convulsing, causing her to slide off. She sits up and watches.

The Caterpillar's body is rippling spasmodically, his many dozens of legs twitching while moving, as if he is trying to run somewhere. His eyes are open wide, staring into space, the hose is still taped to his mouth, but the hose part is broken away from the rest of the hookah.

The Caterpillar flails and convulses and shudders, rolls to his right side on top of the hookah and then he is still.

Alice approaches him to see his face. His eyes are still open wide in terror, but the life seems to have left them. She places her hand over the open end of the hose so that he won't be able to take any more breaths of fresh air, and watches for several minutes.

The Caterpillar doesn't take any breaths, his eyes remain open the whole time.

Finally, she says to him, "Watch out for the spice. That stuff'll kill you."

She searches around a few minutes. The Caterpillar never kept any other possessions than his hookah, and he didn't wear clothes, so he has no pockets to search. Her heart is not here. So she supposes she'll go see the Hatter next.

Wh𝛂t Alice Sees

Alice feels as if someone is toying with her as she stumbles about—it's as if someone is shifting the ground beneath her feet.

She blinks as she looks at the mushroom. "That can't be right," she mumbles, as she stares at it in alarm, for it now seems to be floating in the air upside down. She remembers that often when you invert things, it causes them to become evil. "So is that an evil mushroom?"

She glances at the Caterpillar, then does a double-take, because where the Caterpillar once was, there is now a cocoon. The hookah hose is slithering away like a snake, pulling part of the hookah with it.

She notes that there's much too much bright blue and red in the things she sees, and everything seems to blur and shift.

"Why, this must be a…a…uh…hallucination! Well, time for me to return to my regular size."

She grabs a piece of the right side of the mushroom, taking a guess, because she doesn't know if it being upside down causes its left to become right, and vice versa.

She begins nibbling. She feels her head begin to expand first.

The cocoon is wriggling. It cracks open while Alice is growing. A black butterfly unfurls its wings then flutters off.

"Finally! He seemed to have been stuck in perpetual adolescence! But he grew up way too fast." She giggles. "As am I!" She stops nibbling because she is normal size now.

She stares wide-eyed, because standing in front of her is Humpty Dumpty, but he looks cracked all over like a boiled egg that's been tapped all about by a spoon. She notices he's wonkily-shaped now, not very round, almost cubicle.

Alice says, "Weren't you just a round—"

He scowls. "I've been around, yes, no thanks to you! You stay away from me! The king and his men put me together again, and I'm starting all over again. I'm building a brand new wall I am, in an entirely different spot I am, away from you!"

"But I'm right here! You really couldn't have chosen a worse spot."

"Technicalities. Don't bother me with them." He produces a brick in one hand. "I shall build my wall brick by brick." He sets the brick on the ground then stands on top of it, which proves quite difficult as demonstrated by his teetering and waving and whirling of his arms.

"Whoooa…I'm…whoa…I'm Humpty dum… whoa…Dumpty here on my wall… Ack!…I'm Humpty…whoa…Dumpty and I cannot fall!"

"Why that's not a proper wall. That's just a brick." She suddenly notices that the brick is set on a railroad track. Why hadn't she noticed that before?

"I shall…whoa…build…ack…the wall…higher later."

"And wider too, I should think. By the way, did you know you are standing on railroad tracks? That really is quite a bad location for your wall. What if a train comes?"

"Hush. I'm balancing!"

Suddenly she notices that some distance away, behind Humpty Dumpty, the March Hare and the White Rabbit stand several yards away from each other, facing each other—each is holding a large carrot in their arms.

The White Rabbit shouts at the hare, "I've had enough of you! There's only room for one rabbit in Wonderland!"

The Hare shouts back, "I'm not a rabbit, I'm a hare, you scoundrel!"

They begin hopping toward each other, holding the carrots out like javelins. Both carrots strike true, impaling them both.

Alice cheers, shouts, "Eat your veggies!"

The rabbit and hare, still impaled and bleeding, are shaking hands and bowing after their respectable duel.

Humpty Dumpty says, "What's all that ruckus? Please...whoa...be quiet. I'm trying to balance here."

Alice looks at Humpty Dumpty just in time to see the black butterfly land on the tip of Humpty's nose and rest there.

Humpty's face takes on a comical look of alarm. "Shoo! You!" He is looking down, cross-eyed at the butterfly, which isn't moving.

Alice hears the sound of the train's horn.

She turns to see it in the distance, but it is rapidly approaching, much faster than seems possible.

The March Hare and the White Rabbit are hugging awkwardly, despite the huge carrots stuck in their bodies.

I must knock Humpty Dumpty from the wall so he doesn't get hit by the train! Because I want to be the one who breaks him... again!

The train has almost arrived. The butterfly finally flits off.

Humpty doesn't appear to see the train in his side vision, because of how he has to stand on the brick. "What is that racket? Distracting. I must concentrate on my...whoa...balance!"

"I will break you!" With a howl, Alice runs, jumps up with both feet in front of her, sailing through the air like she is sitting in a chair, knocking Humpty from the wall. He explodes into shimmering swirling confetti sparkles.

She turns her head in midair to see the train slamming right into her.

All of a sudden, she's lying on the ground on her back as if none of that happened. She looks around. She sees the little mushroom, right side up, and the little dead caterpillar next to his hookah.

She stands, dusts herself off, then staggers toward the Mad Hatter's table.

A TEA PARTY

So, Alice makes her way to the tree, where the March Hare, the Hatter and the Dormouse spend much of their time Tea-Partying.

When she is almost there, she yelps in pain from a stinging pain on her arm. She looks down to see several scratch marks along her right arm. They look like the claw marks from some sort of animal.

In panic she crouches, looks all around, but sees nothing. Now she realizes something must have scratched Malice. Alice watches her wounds begin to ooze blood.

She brings a handkerchief out from her pocket and does her best to attend to her wounds. *At least they're shallow.*

She can think of nothing other to do than to continue on her way.

After about half an hour, she can see it. There is a table set out under a tree in front of a house, and the Hatter is having tea at it. The Dormouse is sitting next to him. The Dormouse is as usual, fast asleep, but Alice doesn't see the March Hare, who usually sits to the the other side of the Dormouse.

The Hatter seems to be steadying himself with one hand resting on the Dormouse while he holds a cup of tea in the other. He is blinking rapidly and bugging his eyes out in a most peculiar way.

Alice, still feeling the effects of the spice, giggles at him.

The Hatter says, "Oh, no! Not again. It is quite rude to attend a Tea Party twice! Rude to all the other attendants, you see! Perhaps come back some time when we have some seats available?"

Alice looks around mockingly at the long table which has quite a number of empty chairs. She sees two custard pies just like the ones the Hatter had brought to the party resting on the table amongst all the fine china. She also notices that one of the chairs has been overturned, some of the cups knocked over, the table cloth seems crinkled and ruffled.

Malice must have been here!

Alice takes a seat across from the Hatter, knowing that it might be rude, but she is having a hard time balancing and focusing her eyes on the Hatter at the same time. He always looks mad, but he now appears madder than usual, and he has a long bleeding slash on his forehead.

The Hatter proclaims, "I gave the heart to you like you wanted. It's rude to only *pretend* to leave, don't you think?" He turns to where the March Hare usually sits. "Oh, yes, that's right," he mutters.

"What's right?"

"He ran off after you tussled with him, of course."

"I'm sorry, but that wasn't me. You see, my reflection got separated from me, and well, she looks just like me, only my left side is on her right side, and vice versa. You know what I mean?"

"Like the Tweedles? Great. Just what we need. More twins!"

"Yes, so you gave her the heart?"

"Yes, but she said she doesn't know how to put it back in, whatever that means."

Because she doesn't have the card.

He sets down his tea cup. "Excuse me." He slaps his face. "Get yourself together, man!" He's talking to himself. "Have you gone mad?"

Alice laughs. "I daresay you seem madder than usual."

"Well, of course, you—I mean *she* made me eat my hat! I have a question."

"Yes?"

"Are you sure you weren't just here? Maybe it's some sort of double vision I'm having. Why, I see two of you right now. So if I saw you before is that quadruple vision? Or triple?"

Alice is not about to try to figure out what *that* might mean. "I'm afraid that must just be your eyes. What do you mean, she made you eat your hat?"

"Yes, she rudely burst into our private tea party and started making demands that we hand over the heart I legitimately got from Humpty. She fought with the March Hare, who ran off and she forced me to lick my hat. I protested. The wearing of my hats is no problem, but the licking of them is not at all good. Well, she said she would cut me if I didn't do it. She had a razorblade. And well, what could I do? I'm not a fighter. I prefer to watch the action, rather than dirty my hands with it. Filthy stuff, that action is. Then she took off with the heart, and now I'm probably going to die." He looks mournful.

A bit of sweat rolls down his forehead, mixing with the blood of his wound. He seems to be sweating quite heavily.

Alice says, "Just from licking your hat?"

"Yes, well, she made me lick quite a lot, a lot more than usual. Usually I just bite the brim while I'm shaping my hats, and a wee bit of mercury and chemicals gets in, making me a wee bit mad. It's quite inadvertent. I mean I don't go around licking hats for no reason. Why that would be positively mad, don't you think?" He's trembling now.

Alice says, "You don't look well." She can't help but smile a little, but she has no burning desire to see the Hatter die out of revenge. The Hatter might have been rude at times, but he was more of a nuisance who never engaged in the completely horrible things that the others in Wonderland used to.

The Hatter looks kind of swirly…like a pineapple cactus or something. No, wait, there isn't such a thing. Or maybe there is, in Wonderland. It had been such a long time since she'd lived in the ordinary world where reality followed proper rules. Who knows, maybe if a gardener—

The Hatter clears his throat.

Mary realizes she has been kind of staring vacantly at him.

He says, "May I ask you a question?"

"Okay."

"Why is a raven like a writing desk?"

She rolls her eyes. "I'll tell you later."

"It shouldn't be *too* much later, as I will be inconveniently indisposed being deceased."

Alice can believe that. The Hatter is outright shuddering now.

The Hatter says, "So whose heart was it, anyway?"

Alice shrugs. "I'll tell you, if you tell me what's so special about your hat." He'd always referred to it as his "very special hat", but never said why.

The Hatter sighs. "Very well. There's no point in keeping the secret anymore. And besides, I'm just *dying* to tell you." He chuckles. "Sorry, a little bit of gallows humor. Yes, this my dear, is my voyeur hat. Why, I'm proud to say, I designed it expertly myself! It is exquisite for what it does! All I have to do is tap the top to make it work. Its only limitation is it can only be used three times a day. I can see your expression. What does it do, you wonder."

Alice nods with an encouraging grin.

"Why I use it to watch you, my dear. Though, since I can only use it for short amounts of time, I try to get the timing right so I can view you when you are suffering."

Her smile falters. "Suffering?"

"Yes, all the creative and delicious torments the creatures of Wonderland subject you to. Oh, how I love to watch! To see the exquisite agony on your face, to watch the tears roll down your cheeks, to hear you sob. Oh, you are so exquisitely beautiful in your suffering my dear. And that's why this is the only hat I wear." He gazes into her eyes. "Why you are the most beautifully suffering creature I've ever seen. Why I wish someone would torture you right now so I could witness your beautiful pain one more time before I die." He wipes a bead of sweat from his forehead.

Alice says, "Well, what if *I* were to wear that hat?"

"Well, it's tuned to you, but it would be silly to see yourself, don't you think? Perhaps you would see your twin. Perhaps you could use the hat to get revenge on her? I mean, for my sake. Venge my death, won't you, my dear?"

Alice's grin grows huge. Why, the Hatter looks absolutely wretched at this moment. Why, it seems as if he'll keel over at any instant. There are bits of sparkly pops of light in her vision, but she thinks that must be the lingering effects of the spice.

She waits for him to ask...

"So," he says, "you said you'd tell me." He coughs for several seconds. "So, who's heart was it?" His voice sounds raspy.

"It was mine." As his face registers fear, she nods. "Yes, I'm heartless now."

He nudges the Dormouse. "I say, my man, wake up. There's a little girl you must maul." The Dormouse doesn't respond.

Alice doesn't break her gaze with him. "You're close now, aren't you? You look terrible."

"Yes. But we all go sometime, right?"

She nods. "Fancy a riddle?"

Mournfully he says, "Sure."

"Why is a raven like *my* writing desk?" Alice asks.

"Are you going to tell me? I haven't much time."

"Because they both belong to the past and refer to what will be nevermore. A bit of a stretch I admit, but we both know you never intended the poem to have an answer."

He nods sagely. "Ahhh..." His eyes begin to roll to the back of his head. "I do believe I'll be dying now."

"No wait! One more thing?"

"Yes? Go on then."

She picks up a custard pie, lifts the hat off his head, and smushes the pie into his face. The timing is perfect and he slumps over face down on the table, his face still in the pie tin. He doesn't move, so she assumes he's dead.

She stares at him for several long seconds, then nudges the Dormouse. "Whaddya think of that, aye?"

The Dormouse doesn't respond at all. Usually, he responds a little, in his sleep, then goes on sleeping.

Unsteadily, Alice stands up. She's still quite out of it. She grabs the Dormouse by the back of the head (She misses the first time she tries, but gets it the second), then yanks his head up.

The Dormouse's throat has been slit. Red blood has poured out over his body, but she hadn't seen it till now.

She says, "Well that's a problem, isn't it?" She chuckles. She lets go of the Dormouse's head and it plonks onto the table. She takes the Hatter's hat and sets it atop her own head.

And even though she knows she's inebriated and not thinking straight, she just gives in to the sudden impulse because, why not? After all, she's been wanting to do this for so long, but never had the heartlessness to actually go through with it.

So she pushes the dead Dormouse and Hatter out of their chairs onto the ground. She puts her hands under the edge, then she flips the table, shouting at the top of her lungs, sending china flying.

SHADOW

Underneath her chin, Alice hears a female voice say, "Sickening! Why you ought to be ashamed!"

Alice's eyes bug out comically. She can't see her own eyes, but she can imagine, and the thought makes her giggle. She tries to look under her chin, but peers instead at her chest.

"No dummy!" says the voice. "Down here. On the ground."

Alice looks but only sees...

"Yes," says the voice. "I'm your shadow!"

"Well well well, has my shadow come out to play?"

"I want to speak to you, because I'm outraged by your recent behavior—separating from your reflection and running around. Why it's just not proper!"

Alice blinks. She realizes that the shadow's voice sounds similar to her own, only flatter and less colorful. She stammers, "Well I. Um. I'd like to change that."

"You better! How am I supposed to decide which of you two to be the shadow for? Why, I've been hopping back and forth between you two! I'm so tired!"

Alice and her shadow wipe her brow.

Alice scowls. "Well, pick one! Aren't shadows supposed to be silent? I don't need your attitude."

Alice and her shadow put their arms akimbo and say, "No! This can't go on much longer! Unless you two get back together, I'm leaving you both! Then you'll have *no* reflection and *no* shadow either! I don't think you'll like that, will you?"

Alice's and the shadow's shoulders slump. "I wish I could recombine with Malice, but I don't know how."

Alice and her shadow raise a finger in the air. "I know how. You must both go to the Looking Glass and be reflected by it at the same time. That will undo all of this separateness silliness."

Alice knows where the Looking Glass is. It was the entrance she went through when she first arrived in Wonderland, and she's always dreamed of going back out of Wonderland through it. It's inside a house on an eighth square of the chessboard, guarded by the Jabberwock. She wonders if Malice would voluntarily meet her there just to become a reflection again. "But —"

Alice and her shadow put a fingertip to her lips to quiet her. "Shhh. You're wondering, why would Malice agree to that? Well don't worry. I will convince her. I'll even lie if I have to. I am so sick of this hopping about! So, here's my plan. You make your way to the Eighth Square where the Looking Glass is, and I'll persuade or deceive Malice into doing the same. And hopefully we'll go back to being one big happy family again, and I can go back to being your silent shadow. Agreed?"

Alice and the shadow nod. Now Alice and the shadow each takes one of their hands in the other and makes a hand shake.

"Okay, then," says the shadow. "Let's see what Malice is up to right now. Hold on."

Alice's shadow disappears. It's quite an unnerving occurrence.

Alice doesn't have much time to "reflect" on it though, as it were, before her shadow pops back—for a brief moment, it appears to have kitten ears.

The shadow says, "Oh, you shan't believe this! Malice is going to try to summon the Cheshire Cat. If that hat works, now would definitely be a good time to use it."

Alice and her shadow point to the hat on the ground.

Alice and her shadow put it on and tap the top.

Malice and the Cat

The vision before Alice's eyes shimmers, then suddenly she is gazing at a girl wearing a cat suit. It's as if Alice is hovering slightly above and a short distance away from the girl. The girl is sitting on the ground, in what looks to be an outside area with wooden plank floors. There is a wall made of cobblestones to the right. There are two guillotines behind the girl. It looks a lot like the Queen's execution area where she sends creatures off to be beheaded.

Alice gasps. "Oh! Why, it's as if I'm floating above! Can she see me?"

The shadow answers, "No, she can't. You are watching from afar. I can see all that you see, as well."

"Is that Malice? At the Queen's execution area?"

"Yes, she got the cat suit from the Queen of Heart's tailor. It's glamored to summon and charm the Cheshire

Cat. And she's going to use the catnip too. But I'm afraid I must go now, lest he suspect."

"Lest *who* suspects?"

Alice sees the shadow appear next to Malice on the ground.

Catnip? They say it makes cats really amorous.

Alice observes Malice more. On the ground, next to scurrying rats, is a jar, a ball of yarn, and the pistol. The rats are surrounded by a circle of white chalky substance. Alice assumes it's some of the Queen's special rat poison—the rats, sensing it, would be forced to stay inside the circle.

Malice opens the jar, dips her hand into it, then smears some goopy substance onto her lips through the mask before shouting,

"Here kitty kitty!

Won't you come out and play?

I've got some rats, I've got some yarn,

For you to swat today!"

Malice looks around hopefully for a few moments, but now her shoulders slump.

"Kitty kitty come out and play!

I've decided to shoot myself today!"

The head of the Cheshire Cat materializes in front of Malice. Just the head, as usual. Alice can only see the back of his head from her viewpoint.

Alice feels fright go through her. *If Malice shoots herself, I'll die too!* She shouts "No!" but they don't respond. "Shadow? Shadow stop her! Shadow come back!" None of it works, the shadow remains at Malice's side, so all Alice can do is watch.

"Hello Alice," the cat says to Malice. "My, that is a fetching outfit you have on today. You'd make such a pretty kitty. And what is that? Rats and yarn? Gifts for me?"

"Yes, to thank you for all your help."

"My pleasure, kitten."

Malice takes a deep breath. "Well, here goes." She lifts the pistol, presses it to her temple. "Oh, but first, I'd like to request my customary kiss of death."

The cat grunts in frustration. "What?"

"My kiss of death. Why it's…customary! It's only the polite thing to do."

"Yes, yes," says the cat. "I'm sorry, where are my manners? I daresay it sounds a proper right and fitting thing to do. Well, here goes." The hovering cat head floats to shift to kiss her cheek.

Malice shouts, "Rudeness!"

"I'm sorry, am I doing it wrong?"

"Of course you are. Have you never given a kiss of death before?"

"I'm afraid I haven't."

"Well it's got to be on the mouth! Well?" She shakes the pistol as if to say, "I can't hold this here all day."

"Very well." The cat floats and as far as Alice can tell from her viewpoint, they kiss for several seconds, before the cat head floats back.

The cat says, "Why, your lips are delicious."

"Thank you. Well, here goes."

Alice hopes she isn't about to die as she watches.

Malice pulls the trigger. Alice winces.

But there is no bang. Only the click of the hammer.

Malice pouts cutely. "Gun no go boom."

The cat shouts, "Outrageous! Is the gun broken? Did you fire its shot already?"

Malice shrugs. "Go ask Alice." She points and it looks as if she's pointing right at Alice.

Alice feels a twinge of fright, though her heart, of course, doesn't begin to race.

The cat turns his head, and now Alice can see his face. He's looking without focusing his eyes, his smile is gone. He now looks a bit sleepy, as if too tired to smile. "I don't see her," he says. While he's looking, Malice goes onto all fours. The Cheshire Cat turns back around. "Alice?"

"No, sorry, she left. I'm just an itty bitty kitty, won't you come out and play?"

"You are? You look like—"

"No! I'm an itty bitty kitty!" She purrs. Licks the back of her hand. "Who are you?"

"I'm the Cheshire Cat. I—I feel strange."

"Won't you come frolic with me? I've got yarn, pretty yarn, I've got rats for you today, so won't you come out to play?"

Malice slaps sloppily with her "paw" at the scattering rats. She isn't being serious she seems to be saying, as she grins big at him, tilts her head to the side. She pouts.

"Why, where are your paws? Won't you bring them out so we can play?"

Alice can no longer see the Cheshire Cat's face, but his voice sounds slurry and slow. Was it from the catnip? He says, "I—I can't. I—I can't bring my body out, because the Queen wants to behead me. So I don't want to pop my body onto my head, because if I don't have a body I can't be beheaded. I must be careful."

Malice looks around. "I don't see the Queenie Weenie. Come onnnn. Play with the yarn wif me." She begins swatting the yarn back and forth.

"Ooh, I absolutely adore yarn!" He groans in exasperation. "It's just that I only have one life left. The Queen took the other eight away. I can never let down my guard! She can be so sneaky."

"Oh, poo!" She gives a megapout. "She's not here. It's just me, the rats, and a scaredy cat."

"Awww come on. Don't tease…"

"Here, just hold the yarn in your mouth then, if you aren't gonna bring your claws out."

She stoops and takes the ball of yarn in her mouth as if she's a cat, then sashays up, offering to transfer the yarn to his mouth.

The Cheshire Cat's head flits lightly forward, but Malice bounds a short distance away and sets the yarn down. "Nuh uh. If you want the yarn, you must give me a kiss."

"*Another* kiss, didn't I just give you one? Or didn't I? I feel so confused."

"You didn't give me a kiss. Maybe you just *wished* you did."

"I feel so strange, like I'm drunk. I'm forgetting things even from moment to moment. I'm sorry to be rude, but who are you again?"

"I'm a little kitty kitty.

Tell me, do you think I'm pretty?"

"Yes, very much so."

"Would you like to kiss me? Don't be shy."

"Well—"

"I'll only let you play with my yarn if you give me a kiss," she says in a flirtatious, mock demanding voice.

"Ha ha! Very well! I shall do as the lady kitty commands."

Malice lowers her head slightly as the Cheshire Cat approaches and gently kisses her.

"I say!" he exclaims. "Your lips are as sweet as catnip."

Malice merely smiles then nudges the ball of yarn over to him with her nose.

"Oh my, that is most delectable yarn, the fibers, the most lustrous color. I can tell the craftsmanship in the weaving—it is most exquisite. Rarely have I seen such yarn."

Malice purrs. "Let's play with it together. Let me see your paws, my darling."

"Oh, I can't resist you, my darling kitty! Here! Here are my paws." The rest of his body materializes. He sits on the ground, like a normal cat, as opposed to floating.

They begin to frolic and play. They bat the ball of yarn between them. Then the Cheshire Cat kills a few of the rats, while Malice pretends to swat at some of them—the Cheshire Cat offers the bloody rats to Malice as a gift and she accepts them while taking the opportunity to coax him into two more kisses.

Alice figures that if each kiss was laced with catnip, why the Cheshire Cat must be *quite* inebriated at this point.

Malice coaxes the Cheshire Cat in for another kiss, but just at the last second, she turns away, teasing, then bounds away.

From a distance away, she shouts, "I would very much like to marry you, Cheshire Cat. Do you think I'm being too forward?"

Alice notices that Malice is standing (in the way a four-legged cat stands) behind a block of wood with a semicircular indentation. Above the wood is suspended a silver blade. It's a guillotine, she realizes.

The Cheshire Cat says, slurring a great deal, "No, no, my darling. No, I mean, yes. I've been wanting so much to say that. I mean, marry me, please. I've wanted to say it! Too afraid before. I was, I mean."

"Come then," Malice says, with an enchanting smile. "Prove you mean it. Seal it with a kiss."

"I—I don't know. Something doesn't feel right..."

"What? Do I have to pout?" She pouts. "Super Megapout? How about this? I call it my death pout."

And she unleashes a very grand example of an extreme form of pouting.

"Awww. I could never resist you, my darling Lenore. Yes, I want us to marry you. I mean, marry me." He walks drunkenly toward her.

"Yes, come my darling."

Unsteadily he approaches. She encourages, saying, "Yes, seal it with a kiss." She puckers her lips.

He stops in front of the wooden block and stretches his neck over to kiss her.

While they kiss, Malice's hands move, seeming to pull something—moments later, the blade of the guillotine falls, slicing the Cheshire Cat's head off.

Arterial spray shoots out from his neck, drenching Malice as her lips are still puckered in a kissy face, and the Cheshire Cat's head drops out of view.

Malice wipes the blood from her face while she grins. Her teeth are red with blood.

Now Alice's view of the scene shuts off.

The Queen of Hearts

Alice decides to trust her shadow, and walks toward the Eighth Square, hoping Malice will meet her there.

While walking, she feels a headache come on, and realizes she is no longer under the influence of the spice.

After some time, she hears her shadow again, going pssst.

Alice looks down. "Yes?"

"Malice is about to meet with the Queen! She has it all planned! She's going to use pepper in her eyes. Oh, you won't want to miss this! Oh, I've got to go!"

The shadow again disappears.

Alice taps the top of the hat. Once again, she sees Malice as if she is floating slightly above and a short distance away from her.

Malice is standing where Alice has been many times before, in the Queen's makeup room.

The Queen, though she ruled over the cards, was not a card herself—she was human, though she looked very much like a drawing of a Queen on a card. And she loved to be done-up.

It is one of Alice's scheduled rounds to attend to the Queen and do her makeup. See, the Queen, a few years ago, heard how magical everyone considered Alice's tears to be. Well, the Queen figured her tears could be used to make her appear beautiful. Alice never could tell much difference between before and after the tears spritz, but the Queen always claimed it made her face feel tingly and was absolutely convinced it worked.

Alice watches Malice curtsy. She has shed the catsuit, and is wearing her normal black dress, with no hint of the Cheshire Cat's blood. Things are different than usual. The Queen is sitting in the makeup chair facing away from the mirror rather than looking into it. Also, the Queen is wearing a necklace of hearts, dark red colored and black around the edges. Alice is unable to count how many there are, but it looks like there very well could be thirteen.

"Thank you," says the Queen, "for killing that accursed cat! I'm so glad to have him out of the way. Why, it's one of the few things you've managed to get right."

"You're welcome Your Highness."

"Yes, that's why I've decided to invite you to the ball, just this once. Don't get used to it. But why am I facing this way? Turn me around, you halfwit!"

Malice smiles. "Please. I have something very special in mind. I think it would be so grand if you wait for the surprise!"

The Queen sighs. "Oh very well. I love surprises. Like your surprise birthday party today! Why, I had a grand time at it! But now I have a ball to attend, so I want to look my best. But I want to try something different—exotic, yet elegant, yet splendid, yet inspiring gentle awe, yet inspiring fear of being beheaded. Can you do that?"

Malice claps. "Absolutely, why I'll give you a makeover! And when I'm through, with my special ingredient, I'll give you a brand new face!"

The enthusiasm is contagious and the Queen squeals along. "Ah, it's your tears that make you such a good makeup artist. Without *them* you'd be subpar. But let's have you work your magic, eh! And if I don't like it, I'll have you beheaded."

(The Queen would always threaten Alice with beheading her, but never went through with it, because then where would she get the magic tears?)

So the Queen sits in the makeup chair and Malice gets to work, applying tinctures and powders, drawing with pencils and brushes. She is like an artist who apparently possesses all the same skills as Alice herself.

Malice says, "Done!"

"Ah, now for the finishing touch."

Malice nods, grabs the bottle from the makeup table. The Queen stands, then approaches Malice.

Malice nods, wincing. The Queen slaps her hard across the face then begins launching into her typical insults. "You're a stupid, incompetent, ugly, worthless…" It goes on for several minutes.

Usually, Alice would begin crying now. But that was the old version of Alice with a heart. Malice didn't have one. (Well, at least not an internal one.)

Malice rubs her eyes. Immediately after, Malice's eyes begin to tear up, then the tears begin to roll, copious amounts of tears.

"Boo hoo!" Malice shouts. "Boo hoo! Woe is me!" Alice doesn't think Malice sounds very convincing, but that was to be expected since after all, she has no heart.

The Queen now does what she usually does—she holds the spray bottle to Malice's face to try to capture as many tears in the bottle as she can.

"Excellent!" the Queen proclaims as she screws the cap on.

The usual next events were for Alice to spritz the Queen's face with her tears.

Malice points the bottle nozzle at the Queen's face. "Okay, are you ready to complete your makeover?"

"Oh, yes. I can't wait. Everyone will be so jealous at the ball."

"Are you ready for your brand new face?" Malice says in a teasing voice.

"Oh, hurry up, stupid! Don't make me behead you!" She closes her eyes.

"Okay, here goes." Malice spritzes, applying a fine mist all over the Queen's face. Swivels the chair around. "Okay, open your eyes!"

"Hey, how come you don't have a reflection? Oh, I can feel the tingling. It's warm, warmer than usual. Hey, it's hot!"

The skin of her face begins to bubble and smoke. "What? It burns! It ahhh!"

She stands, begins clawing at her face. Her face is smoking quite a bit now, and the Queen seems to be tearing at the flesh of her face. She falls to the ground and curls in a ball, sobbing.

Malice laughs. "Have fun at the ball! Somehow I suspect I'm no longer invited." She exits the room.

Alice's view of the scene shuts off.

ALICE AND HER SHADOW

Her shadow once again garners her attention as she's walking, giving forth a pssst, then "So I did my part."

Alice looks down, says, "Did Malice kill the Queen?"

"Hmm? No, of course not! She's just horribly disfigured. Malice didn't want to kill the Queen—she wanted her to suffer for her crimes."

"So, what? She has a sense of justice now?"

"Hmm? No, just a sense of humor. But I want to tell you I'm fed up with you two being separate, so I'm here to tell you I'm staying away until you get re-smushed-together."

"So is Malice going to meet me at the Looking Glass House?"

"Yes, I told you I did my part. She said to tell you she's looking forward to being recombined."

"Yeah, but the Eighth Square is guarded by the Jabberwock, and they say he kills all intruders with his vorpal blade."

"Yes, but remember, you have the card."

"The card? How will that help me with a jabberwock?"

"Remember his gambling addiction…"

"Of course, everyone knows about it. They say that's why he stole the Queen of Heart's tarts all that time ago—to pay off some debts. So what of it?"

Alice and her shadow tap the side of her head in a *come on, think* mocking motion. "And you still have the Thirteen of Heartless card…"

"That's right," says Alice. "And…"

"Annnd…did the Jabberwock ever confess to stealing the tarts?"

Alice rolls her eyes. "Of course not. I used to naively think he was innocent, but everybody knows he did it, but he never confessed and they've never been able to prove it. They convicted the Knave of Hearts instead."

"Yeah, so…"

"Yeah?" Alice still didn't get it.

The shadow says, "All the jabberwocks come from a proud warrior culture. Don't they say they live by the sword, die by the sword?"

"Yes. So you want me to kill the Jabberwock with his vorpal blade?"

The shadow sighs. "In a way. Tell me, what is the punishment for every crime in jabberwock society?"

Alice thinks for a moment. "Hara kari by their own vorpal blade! It's an honor thing. If they don't do it, they would be disgraced! Hari kari is where they take their own vorpal blade and cut through their stomach to kill themselves."

"I know what it is! I'm your shadow, remember?"

Alice and her shadow cross their arms. Alice says, sounding a bit hurt, "So you want me to prove he stole the tarts?"

"Yes, well, I want you to make the Jabberwock confess to stealing the tarts, which is even better because a jabberwock is bound by honor never to lie."

"Well that's a dumb plan, because he's never confessed before."

"Arggh!" the shadow cries out. They put their hands to the sides of their heads in exasperation. "That's why you gotta use the card! Do you remember its rule for poker?"

Alice tries to think, her mouth shifting from side to side. "Not really. I remember it was a strange rule."

"Ugh! Am I the only one who's been paying attention around here?"

Alice and her shadow shrug.

"Fine!" says the shadow. "Here's the rule:

If him you are dealt when poker's the game,
Your opponents must fold then confess,
The one thing they feel is their own greatest shame,
Because he's the Thirteen of Heartless!

"Now I leave it up to you two from here. I'm sick of you both! Oh, how I long to go back to being just a simple, silent shadow of a single Alice!"

The shadow disappears just as Alice is saying, "Where are you going?"

Alice is thinking that next, she will take the card from her pocket and try to rouse it into speaking again. But when she takes him out and shakes him, he merely giggles—nothing more.

She taps the top of her hat and sees Malice again, but Malice is just walking, so it's not very interesting.

So Alice continues onward, and soon she sees the Jabberwock ahead and approaches him.

JaBBerWockY

"Hidy ho", he says. He smiles a fanginous grin.

I don't know if you know, but jabberwocks are quite frightening creatures, two times taller than the average thirteen-year-old girl, with veiny wings and sharp dripping fangs and long razor-sharp claws. Plus a barbed tail to boot. Horrible, nightmarish monsters, they are.

Alice curtsies. "Hello."

"It's a pleasure to see you again, Alice."

"Well, um, thank you."

"You're welcome. So how would you like to die? Vorpal blade?" He wiggles it in his claw. "Claws?" He crinkles his free claw. "Jaws?" He clacks his teeth together twice. "You know, by the way, that's a very lovely hat."

"Oh," she says flirtatiously. "Fancy a game of poker over it?"

"A game of poker? Why you're just a little girl."

She puts the tip of her finger to the side of her mouth. "Yes, just a little bitty girly compared to you. Why, you aren't gonna kill me are you? It hardly seems fair."

"Awww." He sets the blade down. "I was just trying to scare you a little. Really, as long as you don't try to cross the line of the Eighth Square, we can be nice and friendly."

"But if I try?"

"I'd have to kill you. It's my job. You know…" He sighs. "Us jabberwocks have really been given a bad rap, always portrayed as rampaging monsters who go around killing for no reason. It all has to do with that silly poem. But we are really a proud and honorable species. We don't go around killing innocent creatures." He makes a creepy funny attempt at a smile. "Or innocent little girls. For no good reason, that is."

Alice grins at him angelically and looks cute. "I'm innocent. Are you?"

His creepy grin falters some. "Pardon?"

"No pardon, that's the point. You say you're honorable, but you've never confessed to stealing the tarts. But if you confessed, would you do the honorable thing?"

"Of course. I'd perform seppuku with my own vorpal sword."

"Hari kari?! So let me get this straight. If I can get you to confess today, you will kill yourself? You wouldn't just kill *me?*"

"No. Absolutely not. That would be dishonorable."

"You wouldn't wait for your day at trial? They never filed charges right?"

"I wouldn't wait, because we all know what the verdict'd be. My confession would be irrefutable evidence, for jabberwocks are *sooo* honorable that they are incapable of lying. And the Queen's court doesn't allow 'hari kari' as you so inaccurately call it—they'd want to behead me by guillotine. And dying that way would be...dishonorable."

"Well, if jabberwocks are *soooo* honorable, well, help me understand. Why would one of them commit the crime of stealing the tarts, hypothetically speaking?"

"Well, hypothetically maybe a jabberwock might have debts and didn't realize taking the tarts was such a serious offense and thought the tarts were free for the taking. But he should have known better than to think that bitch of a queen could be so generous."

"I see," Alice says. "So did you steal the tarts?"

The Jabberwock sighs. "I assert my right to remain silent on that matter."

She decides to use her newfound skill of lying. Despite the fact that the old version of herself always thought he was a secret sweetheart, she says, "Well I must *confess,* you certainly seem more pleasant than I imagined. I always see you at my unbirthday parties, but I've always been intimidated by you and your blade."

"Oh, I'm not so bad, am I?"

"Well you're not like the others. You always stand back. Never participate."

"Oh I like to watch them torment you. They come up with such creative ways!"

"Isn't that dishonorable?"

"Hey, as long as I'm not the one doing it, what's the harm?" He shrugs.

Alice shrugs too, now grins. "Okay, one last question before we get down to playing cards. Why do you guard the Eighth Square?"

"Well no one in Wonderland wants you to escape or become a queen. That would ruin all the fun. So I guard it to keep you out."

"Become a queen?"

"Yes, if you ever were to enter an eighth square, you'd become a queen. Hey, you know, I think I'd really like a game of poker right now."

Alice nods, reaches into her dress for the pack of cards. "Shall we play?"

"Oh, let's! I do so love playing cards!"

Alice sits cross-legged in the grass and begins to shuffle. She hopes she is dealt the Thirteen of Heartless, but she doesn't know how to cheat, so she just shuffles the way she normally would. She remembers the Thirteen of Heartless saying something about how he could show up in a deck anywhere he wanted to.

Let's hope so.

The Jabberwock sets his blade down and mimics sitting cross-legged in front of her.

She can't help but giggle and make a mocking wriggle at him. "Why, you look so dainty sitting that way!"

Alice doesn't know if jabberwocks can blush, but she thinks he almost does. He says, "Well, anything for a bit of a game."

Something occurs as she shuffles. "You know, I heard that when one commits hari kari, there is someone with a sword who beheads them right after they slice their tummy. Is that true?"

"Yes, they're called the 'second'. They do it to relieve the suffering, because the pain can be excruciating."

"My, that's a big word! But isn't it cheating?"

The Jabberwock looks outraged and offended. "It most definitely is not! It is completely honorable. Why, a jabberwock would *never* cheat! Why *cheating* is…why it's a terrible thing to do! I'm offended you should even *think* that!"

"Okay, okay. Sorry! Let's play shall we? Put the pot in." She sets her hat on the ground between them. "What you got?"

The Jabberwock digs in a pouch on a strap at his side. "Three, four, five gold coins? Is that satisfactory?"

Alice nods, then the Jabberwock adds it to the pot.

Alice says, "Now, cut the deck." She holds the deck out to him. "I'm sorry that the cards are so small compared to your, you know, humongous razor sharp claws."

"Oh, it's okay. I'm quite dexterous. It's just my eyes that are the problem. You'll see when you get my age."

"You use big words." (She really doesn't think the words are that big, but she's practicing her deception skills.)

Amazingly, he manages to use the tips of his claws to cut the deck.

As she deals five cards to each of them, Alice makes small talk. "So, if I crossed the line to the Eighth Square, would you enjoy killing me?"

"Oh, very much so. Little girls have so much red inside of them. You don't notice until you bring it out of them."

"Ah, I never really thought about it that way."

"That's because you're a prissy, innocent little girl." He takes the five cards in his claws. The cards are rather tiny in comparison to his claws. It's amazing that he can manage to hold them so well. "Hold on a second." He rummages again in his pouch, brings out a pair of spectacles and puts them on. "It's the eyes that are the problem, you see."

Alice nods supportively.

She looks at her own hand. She has four jokers and the Ace of Spades. There isn't a Thirteen of Heartless, which is what she wants, so she turns in four cards, so she'll get four back.

The Jabberwock turns in zero cards. She peers at him, but his poker face is inscrutable. Despite the fact it doesn't help her game, she likes his poker face, because it doesn't reveal his scary fangs.

Alice looks at the four cards she's been dealt back. The Thirteen of Heartless is amongst them, the others are two jokers and the Ace of Spades. So it turns out the Thirteen of Heartless is capable of cheating after all, not that she minds.

She shouts, "I have the Thirteen of Heartless! That means you have to fold and confess!"

She isn't sure what's supposed to happen next, but what does happen is that the Thirteen of Heartless begins to glow.

In a dazed voice, the Jabberwock says, "I fold. I had five jokers. But what's this about confessing?"

As she gathers the cards up, she says, "Yes, is there something you'd like to tell me?"

A look of exquisite perturbation comes over the Jabberwock's face. He tries to fight it for several more seconds, but finally he blurts, "Okay, I stole the Queen's tarts, okay? I confess!"

With a condescending pout, Alice says, "Well, you know what happens now. You must do the honorable thing."

"Yes," he says. He bows his head. He scooches his glasses up, now picks up the vorpal blade.

Does he not realize he doesn't need the glasses anymore? Perhaps I should tell him, she thinks, but she doesn't want to break his momentum. She slips the deck into her pocket.

The Jabberwock meanwhile kneels in the grass, with the vorpal blade laid out in front of him. Alice stands in front of him, watching the ceremony with a big grin on her face.

The Jabberwock begins to recite his poem.

The Jabberwocky code has made,
Us conduct ourselves with honor.
We live and die by our own blade,
So soon, I shall be a goner.

I kneel today in loathsome shame.
I'm fully confessing my crime.
And for this dishonour to my name,
It's hari kari time.

The Jabberwocky creed, it is firm,
Every sentence the same, there's just one:
To wriggle my guts like a worm,
For soon with my blade they'll be spun!

I stole the tarts, it now is clear,
Beyond any and all disavowal.
So with my vorpal blade, I fear,
It's time to disembowel!

One two! One two! Now a fatal boo boo,
By my own vorpal blade has been done!
And now with a stir that's so fast it's a blur.
Ow, see how my entrails are spun!

I feel so much pain as I'm dying,
I ask of you, behead me please!
I see now that you are not crying,
But I beg of you here on my knees!

Delicately, the Jabberwock transfers the sword by its bloody handle to Alice. It is dripping all over red.

Now Alice decides to make up some poetry, recalling the old *Jabberwocky* poem and mimicking a stanza.

"And will I slay the Jabberwock?
Death by *my* hands, a coocoolicious girl!
O frabjuous day! Callooh! Callay!
I chortle as I whirl!"

Alice spins in order to give force to her blow. The Jabberwock is upright, exposing his neck for her. When she whirls completely back around, blade out, there is no *one two*—there is only *one,* as the vorpal blade slices cleanly through the Jabberwock's neck. His head flings off to the side and the neck stump gushes with blood.

Alice is quite satisfied with herself. She is after all, not a skilled swordsman. She watches the body twitch until it is still. She looks to the Jabberwock's head—its eyes are still open, but staring dead.

She throws the blade to the ground, then inspects her hands, covered in blood.

"Ooh icky!" she proclaims with wrinkled nose.

She does her best to clean her hands, puts the hat back on.

She hears a crunching sound and looks down to see that she has stepped on the Jabberwock's glasses. "Oopsy! You'll have to schedule an appointment with the optimist or you shan't be able to read!"

She looks over at the Jabberwock's head.

"Oh, don't look at me like that. If you didn't want them stepped on, you shouldn't have left them lying about."

The Jabberwock doesn't respond.

Alice walks toward the outer edge of the Eighth Square. Just before she enters, she tries again, saying, "Shadow? Shadow are you there?" But the shadow doesn't appear. She shrugs, then steps over.

Showdown

Alice crosses the outer line of the Eighth Square. As she does, she feels a sudden weight atop her head. She discovers that there is a crown *underneath* her top hat. "Of all the curious headgear!" she exclaims. "Imagine wearing two hats at once, when one of them would do! It's unfitting for a queen, if that's what I am now."

She taps the top of her hat but has no vision of Malice. "This thing doesn't work, anyway."

So she takes off the hat and holds it in her hand and is satisfied with just the crown on her head. And now she enters the Looking Glass House and looks around. It's been so long since she's been in here, but it's like she last left it, except much dustier.

Perhaps I should dust it as I wait. I do hope I don't have to wait too long.

When she walks into the room where the looking glass is, the room looks like an ordinary room, with the looking glass on the wall. There's the clock on the mantelpiece. There's the table with the chess board on it and its pieces.

She almost doesn't want to, but she looks into the mirror. She has no reflection. She first came to Wonderland through the mirror, and she wonders if she can leave through it as well. But when she presses her fingertip to its surface, she finds it's just a solid, regular mirror. Perhaps when she had a heart, that might have made her cry, but the tears don't come. All she knows is that she must get her reflection and her heart back, but she can't really remember why.

She sighs. "This place is a mess! Is there a duster about?"

There is a cabinet set against one of the walls—as she's opening it and peering inside, she sees there are a couple of books and an old stopwatch. She is just about to investigate these curious relics when she hears someone call out behind her, "I hope I'm not too late... for your unhappy birthday party."

Alice turns around to see Malice standing in the doorway. Malice is also wearing a crown, holding the bloody vorpal sword in one hand and a large blue cloth sack in the other.

Alice says, "Malice. Welcome. What's in the sack?"

"It's a surprise for later, for your unhappy birthday party."

"You mean our *happy* birthday party."

"Oh yeah, right."

"So my shadow told me you've decided to recombine with me in the mirror?"

Malice nods. "Absolutely. And I brought our heart too. The Mad Hatter had it, the jerk. But I gave him a little justice."

Alice nods. She points. "The magic Looking Glass is over there. If we get reflected by it at the same time, we'll come together again, just like before."

Malice looks. "Yes, I can't wait. I just want things to be the same as before. Less complicated that way. But first, we have to deal with the heart."

"Hmm? Why not recombine first and then deal with the heart?"

Malice rolls her eyes. "Are you stupid? You need to play the game using the card to get your heart back, right? You can't play by yourself. That wouldn't work, right?"

"Wouldn't it?" Alice isn't sure.

"Well, of course not. You need someone else to play with. Our shadow explained it to me. The order of events has to be, put the heart in first, *then* recombine in the Looking Glass."

"But only one of us can win the heart. How will that work?"

"Well, my dumb twin, that's how games work right? There's a winner and a loser." She rolls her eyes. "Trust me, it'll work. Just one of us needs to win the heart, then in the looking glass mirror, it'll make us the same again…it'll make us mirror reflections."

"Are you sure?" Alice asks.

Malice nods. "Absolutely. Trust me?"

"Well, sure. You're me, kind of. Gotta trust myself, right?"

Malice nods. "Right."

Alice sets the top hat open end up on the table next to the chess board. "So the game will be—"

Malice interrupts. "Yeah yeah our shadow told me all about it. If one of us tosses the Thirteen of Heartless in the hat, that person will be able to put our heart back in. Let's play! It's only a matter of time before someone makes it."

Malice reaches into her sack and pulls out a wooden heart-shaped box. There are still objects inside the sack. Malice opens the box to show the heart to Alice.

It looks like a cartoon version of a red heart, but around the edges, it's turning black.

Malice, seeing her expression, explains, "It gets blacker the longer it's left out. But don't worry. It will probably recover once it's in the proper place inside one of our chests!"

Alice says, "Yes, that's where it has to go. I'm sure there must be a good reason to have a heart. After all, many had to die to recover it, so I suppose we should get to it."

Malice grins, says, "Exactly."

So they get to work taking turns tossing the Thirteen of Heartless at the hat. After half a dozen times or so, Alice finally makes it. "Ha! You lose."

Malice just sticks her tongue out playfully.

Alice picks the heart up out of its box. She's still holding the card, which begins to glow with a white light. Not quite knowing what to do, she presses the hand holding her heart onto her chest.

Her hand begins to go into her chest, as if she's pressing it into a reflection of herself on top of water. She feels no pain, only a soothing warmth.

"It's working!" Alice shouts.

"Wonderful!" Malice shouts.

When Alice's hand reaches the point in her chest she thinks a heart should be, she lets go. She feels the heart twist, shift inside her, settle into place. She pulls her hand out. She places her hand atop her chest and she smiles big as she feels her heart beating.

She raises her head to look at Malice, but before she entirely lifts her chin, she feels a hard blow to the side of her head, almost knocking her off her feet. She shouts in surprise.

She stands dazed for a few seconds, dizzy. She feels her hand jerked down and she falls to the ground. Before she can get her bearings, she feels another blow to her head.

Now she feels as if her hands are being held behind her, hears clanking sounds. She can offer no resistance, stunned as she is. "What?—" She raises her head to see

Malice grinning down at her, holding keys in front of her.

Malice says, "I bet you're wondering what's going on."

Alice just stares stupidly, still dazed.

Malice says, "Well, I just knocked your head about a couple of times, then while you were out of it, I chained your hands to the table leg there."

Alice pulls at her wrists, but they're bound behind her. She hears the tinkle of metal chains. "Why?"

"Why? I'll tell you why. First, as to this card." She holds it up for Alice to see, then rips it in half—the card shrieks pitifully. Malice tosses the two halves of the card in opposite directions.

"Why did you do that? He did you no harm!" Alice feels tears well up in her eyes and begin to roll down her cheeks. At the same time, she kind of feels that the card was funny when it shrieked like that.

Malice looks down at her disdainfully. "Eww. That's gross. I had to make myself cry recently. Had to use peppers in my eyes. Never again. But you, with your *heart*. Why you seem to cry on a dime! If only I had a dime!" She rolls her eyes.

Alice tries to discreetly test her chains, but they tinkle.

Malice says, "I wouldn't try." She tosses the keys on the ground, then lifts the vorpal blade from the table top. "I'll kill you with no remorse if you try to escape. I'm quite heartless, unlike *you*. But then again, your heart is partially blackened, so that should prove interesting."

Alice doesn't know whether to risk trying to fight her way out or not, but then she remembers. "But if you cut me, you cut yourself. We're mirror images."

"Dummy! When I knocked you upside your head, did I knock *me* *on* the noggin too?" At Alice's blank expression, Malice answers, "No, I didn't. Once you got the heart, we ceased being mirror images. Why, I could kill you if I wanted, and it wouldn't affect me. And you know what? I planned this all along. That's why I let you win on purpose in the hat tossing game. I'm more clever than you, you see. Besides, who would actually want a heart anyway? So inconvenient." She's beaming with pride. "And maybe having a *black* heart is worse than having no heart at all!"

"What do you mean by that?"

"Nothing. Oh, well I guess you'll see, won't you? I might just let you live to watch it torment you. They poison the soul."

Alice starts trembling. She definitely doesn't want to die. Meekly she says, "What do you want?"

"You mean, why am I not killing you right now? I'll tell you in a sec. But first, I have prezzies for your unhappy birthday party!" She does her best to clap while holding the vorpal blade. She backs away, kneels, reaches her free hand into the sack.

Meanwhile, Alice is wondering if she might slip the chain off the table leg, then rush Malice, but she has that blade. Or maybe she could reason with her, or maybe Malice has some reason to keep her alive...

Malice pulls the Jabberwock's head out of the sack. "Behold! Scary monster! You did this!"

Alice feels remorse wash over her. "I—that wasn't me. I mean, I was heartless then." She recalls stepping on the Jabberwock's glasses and stifles a giggle. *That's so wrong to think like that. What's wrong with me?* Remorse comes over her again.

"Wo ho ho! I wouldn't have believed it! But having a heart really makes you all sorry and regretful and stuff? Wow! I mean, whoa! I just had to see it with my own eyes, before I kill you. Oh, but I have another gift."

Alice feels more tears rolling down her face. *Did she just say she was going to kill me? Should I make a last ditch effort to try to save my life?*

Malice pulls another head from the sack. She is holding it by the top, presenting it to Alice. It's the Cheshire Cat's head.

The cat's head yawns, but Malice can't see. Malice says, "Now this is a grand trophy. I want to make a collection of heads."

The cat's head opens its eyes, sees Alice and the grin widens on its face.

Meanwhile, Malice says, "Before I kill you, I want you to realize just how clever I was in killing this guy. And I *did* kill him. He only had one of his nine lives left. And me and the Queen of Hearts—"

The body of the Cheshire Cat materializes beneath his head, then twists in a blur. Alice sees red claw marks sprout on Malice's face, going from her temple to across her eyes. She shrieks, drawing back, striking out with the blade that connects solidly with the front shoulder of the cat. The cat crashes to the ground and lies bleeding. He stands and hisses at Malice.

Malice, her face now bleeding profusely, still holding the blade, seems to consider for several long moments what to do next, before she flees out through the door of the hut. She shouts, "This isn't over!"

The cat says, "I think she's gone."

Alice says, "I thought you used up your nine lives."

"Well, I suppose I must have miscounted. Did it take me long to come back to life?"

"Nah. I think you chose the right moment."

"Thanks I think. It's been a strange day. I met a hot kitty today. And next thing I know, I'm here."

With a crazy laugh, Alice says, "Strange?! Why yes, I'll say it's strange! Imagine a world where one's own reflection tries to kill you, and cats *actually* have nine lives! Why it is a world that could only exist in a dream!" She shuts her eyes tightly. "Why this must all be a dream!"

She opens her eyes to see the Cheshire Cat's head floating woefully in front of her. "I'm afraid not, my Queen."

Alice wipes a tear from her cheek. "Maybe I can go back through the Looking Glass?"

"Maybe."

"Even though I don't have a reflection."

The cat shakes his floating head. "Well, no, you can't go through the mirror if you don't have a reflection, my Queen. But the good news is that now you *are* a queen."

Alice sighs, now it suddenly strikes her—the realization of what she has done, the characters she killed, when she didn't have a heart. She feels overwhelmed with sorrow and guilt and the tears well up and flow down her face, dripping on the ground.

But despite the sorrow, she is so grateful to have her heart back, and a part of her feels it really was pretty funny the various ways she killed all those characters.

But no, I mustn't think that way.

She spies the keys lying on the ground. She rattles her chains. "Can you help me get out of these things?"

"Yes, Queen Alice."

62491013R00080

Made in the USA
Middletown, DE
22 January 2018